A.R.P. GIRLS

PATRICIA A MCBRIDE

Created with Vellum

JUNE 1940

'Two days! Two days! Is that all the leave we get after narrowly escaping the Nazis in Paris?' I couldn't believe my ears or that the army would treat us that badly.

Bronwyn and I only landed in Dover the day before. With some other telephonists who'd been working with the British Expeditionary Force in Paris, we'd had a long and at times terrifying journey across country to get to Cherbourg. We just made it five minutes before the last boat left. And now we were being told we could only have two days leave.

Bronwyn put her hands on her hips. 'I'm going to say something serious now,' her lovely Welsh accent tempered by the death looks she was giving the man, 'that's just plain not fair. How're we supposed to replace our uniforms and see our families in two days? Anyway, where are we being posted?'

He shrugged his shoulders and looked down at the papers he'd been shuffling since we stood in front of him. It was a wonder he could find anything, his desk was such a mess of papers and dirty cups.

'Can't help you there, girls. Don't shoot me, I'm just the

messenger. There's a war on and the country needs you, as they say. You're to report to this address at 3pm in two days time.' He thrust a piece of paper into my hand. It was an address in central London.

'How're we supposed to get there? We've only got francs and no-one will take them.'

He opened a drawer and took out two envelopes. He handed us one each. 'You'll find your travel documents, ration cards and some money in there. Should be enough for you to get by on.'

No matter how much we pressed him, he wouldn't or couldn't tell us anything else. In any case, we were simply too tired to argue with him. We longed for a hot bath and a comfortable bed.

'Come on,' I said to Bronwyn as we left his office, 'there's a cafe we passed on the way here, let's get a cuppa while we wait for our train.'

There were new posters since we'd left England months before.

Air Raid Wardens Wanted,

Together we shall strangle Hitlerism,

The more you keep information under your hat, the safer he'll be under his!,

Keep a pig. Join the Pig club!

'I'd like to see my mum getting a pig,' Bronwyn said, 'our back yard's shared with five other families and it's a lot smaller than a pig sty. Mind you, with one lavvy for us and the house next door it smells just as bad.'

The station cafe was crowded and noisy and smelt of damp clothes and sweaty bodies. We fought our way to a table in the corner, bashing against people and bags all the way through. About half of them were in uniform and most of the others were with them, probably family members saying sad goodbyes. The scene reminded me of where Edward had proposed to me, in a station cafe a few minutes before we went off to our separate wars. I was just joining the ATS for training, and he was going back to his posting. I hadn't seen him since.

'I'll fetch the drinks and things,' I said, 'but you'll have to pay me back. Not enough in these envelopes otherwise.'

I went to the counter to fetch two teas and bath buns. The girls were rushed off their feet with so many people to serve. Dirty crockery was piled in the sink and a girl who couldn't have been more than twelve glanced and me and quickly dried her chapped hands on a tea towel that had seen better days.

'Two teas and two bath buns, please,' I said.

'Only two bath buns left, you're in luck.' she said, putting them on a plate and reaching over for the big tin teapot. She was only a slip of a thing and she could barely lift it. Half the tea ended up in the saucers.

'Sorry.' she said, moping up the spills.

I staggered back to the table with the tray, almost tripping over a dog on the way. A soldier saw me and hurriedly took the tray off me. 'There you go, love,' he said, putting it down at our table, 'hope we're going in the same direction.'

I thanked him and turned away, far too tired to flirt.

Bronwyn and I tried to talk but were constantly interrupted by the station announcements which neither of us could understand.

I cut my bath bun in four, trying to make it last longer. Gone were the days when you got jam and cream with them sadly. I took a bite and loved how familiar it was, reminding me of home and how long it was since I'd seen Mum and all my friends. 'Don't know about you Bronwyn, but I'm going to miss them croissants and pastries we had in Paris.'

She nodded, 'They got harder to get though, didn't they. Didn't see any pastries the last few weeks. It was hard enough to find bread.'

She was right. The German army was moving south through France and thousands of refugees flooded Paris trying to escape their clutches. They all needed food and there was never enough to go round. There'd even been talk of food rationing like we had at home.

'You and me are going to be in London, Bronwyn. Fancy finding somewhere to live together?'

She stirred her tea and smiled, 'I do, I really do, but what if we're posted on opposite sides of London?'

I hadn't thought of that. 'I suppose we could try it and if it didn't work out, we'd have to find somewhere separately. We could start looking straight away.'

She pulled a face. 'One bit of luck is two days isn't enough to go back home to Swansea. It's like this, I'd have share a bed with three little ones, kicking me in the back and farting all night. I swear, I never want to be that poor again. My mum is completely worn out, looks twenty years older than she is.' she shook her head, 'What will you do for your two days?'

I bit my lip, 'I suppose I'll go to see Mum, stay there the night and then be back in time to meet you at the office. Where will you sleep if you're not going home?'

She shook her head, 'I don't know, but I'll find somewhere. Don't worry about me.'

My train arrived first and after hugging Bronwyn so tight it was a wonder she didn't have broken ribs, I got on my train, gulping back tears.

I struggled through the hoards of people already on board and several times said, 'Excuse-moi' by mistake, earning myself a few hard looks. Strange because all the time we were in France, I'd never started to think in French, yet here I was slipping into it by mistake.

'Mind the doors, ladies and gentlemen!' The guard shouted at my home station. It all looked strange after so long away, but that didn't stop me hoping to see Mum or one of my friends waiting for me. Crazy because no-one knew I was coming. I stood for a minute taking in the scene, and got an eye full of smoke and bits from the train engine. The station looked the same, the small flowers borders were bright and colourful and everything was neat and tidy. The guard looked well past retirement age, probably bought back to work with so many men away fighting. I wiped my face with my hankie and picked up my rucksack, looking forward to the walk home, past all the places I'd known for so long.

It was a cloudy day with the threat of rain in the air. But that didn't dampen my mood and I walked with a spring in my step. Creamy clematis climbed up the wall of one old house I passed, its flowers so heavy it looked as if they might tumble to the floor any minute. Gardens blushed with Lupins and Philadelphus and other flowers I didn't know the name of. I passed people cleaning their windows or scrubbing their front door step. A couple of lucky people had cars parked outside their house and one man was busy washing his, soap-suds up to his elbows. They all looked up and waved as I walked by.

The cinema where I'd risen to the dizzy heights of assistant manager looked just the same and I saw they were showing *21 days* with Vivian Leigh and Laurence Olivier. I popped my head in the door, but the kind manager wasn't on duty so I didn’t stop. I walked past the Roxy dance hall where me and my friend Jean used to go and smiled at the memories of dancing to big band numbers. But at last I turned the corner into our street. It's a fairly new estate, built by the Corporation to encourage people to move to the town to work in the car factory. Our two bedroomed terrace house with a bathroom and electricity wasn't a palace but compared to what we'd had before, it was heaven. No outside toilets, no chamber pots under the bed, no tin bath in the kitchen on Friday nights. And best of all, no dad. He'd run off with his fancy woman just before I signed up and good riddance to him, nasty bully that he was.

I got out my key but somehow couldn't bring myself to use it unless mum wasn't in. I felt like a stranger in my own home. I knocked instead. I wanted to see her face when she saw me. After a few minutes I knocked again, my spirits sinking. All this way, and she was out.

But just as I was about to give up, the door opened.

By Mum's old boyfriend, Alex, who she said she'd finished with.

The one who tried to get fresh with me when she wasn't looking.

He was tucking his shirt into his trousers and had no shoes and socks on.

I looked up the stairs and Mum was coming down, hair a mess, calling, 'Who is it?'

Pushing past Alex without a word, I stepped forward, 'It's me, mum.'

She flew down the stairs and gave me the biggest hug I'd ever had in my life. 'Lily, Lily, I can't believe it's you.' She pushed me to arms length. 'You look tired. Why didn't you tell us you were coming? I'd have put out banners and made your favourite tea.'

We walked into the kitchen, followed by Alex, who leaned against the sink as if he owned the place. I ignored him.

'I couldn't let you know, I didn't know myself until this morning.'

'Aren't you going to put the kettle on for your daughter?' Alex asked, with a smirk.

'Why don't you put it on.' I replied.

'Woman's work,' he said running his hand through his Brylcreme'd hair, 'anyway, your mum likes looking after me, don't you, love?' He patted her bottom, 'Looks after me upstairs and down, if you get my drift.' He bent over and massaged her shoulder for a minute. My heart pounded as I fought to control my anger.

Mum got up and put the kettle on the ring, then got out the teapot and cups and saucers. 'Wherever have you been, Lily? We haven't heard a peep from you. I've been so worried.'

'I'd love to tell you mum, but you know we can't say anything about our work. But I've had a lot of fun and met people I'd never have met if I hadn't joined the ATS.'

Alex grunted, 'Leaving your old mum behind, are you? Think you're better than us?'

I glared at him, 'I didn't say that at all, stop twisting my words.'

Mum poured the water into the pot, placed the knitted cosy on it and put it with the cups, saucers and little jug of milk on the table. 'I'm sorry not to have any biscuits to offer you, love. It's the rationing.'

'You got your ration book, Lil?' Alex asked, 'Can't expect your mum to feed you without.'

I ignored him. 'I'm only here for one night, Mum. I've got a new posting in London and I start the day after next.'

Her face fell. 'Oh no, and after all this time, I want to spend more time with you.'

'Perhaps Alex can leave so we can spend some time alone.'

Mum went pink and didn't say anything, avoiding my eye.

Alex put his hand firmly on her arm, 'Your mum loves having me here. We're a family, us three. We can spend your leave together like.'

He was never going to be my family, but I bit my lip, not wanting to cause a fight when my time home was so precious.

Just then we heard the first patter of rain. 'Oh dear,' mum said, 'I'll just go and get the washing in. You two sit and chat. No point in us all getting wet.'

No sooner had she left the kitchen than Alex turned to me. 'I knew you'd come back; can't resist me can you? Been up to naughty things while you've been away, have you? I bet you've learned a thing or two.'

I stood up and pushed the chair behind me, 'Shut up, you...'

'I know how to please women. Your mum likes to sit with her legs open across my lap so I can diddle with her. I bet you'd like that too.'

I stepped forward and slapped him hard across the face. Then I picked up his teacup and threw the remains at him.

He stood still for a minute wiping his jumper with a teacloth, then grinned, 'I do like a woman with a bit of spirit. Your mum's a bit too, you know, passive sometimes. A good fight gets to blood going to all the right places. You and me'd be good together.'

I pushed past him and went to the garden. Mum had to know what he was like. I'd kept quiet about it last time he tried it on with me, but this was just too much.

But he followed me out and I knew he'd deny anything I said.

'I've got to go, mum.' I said, 'I've just remembered somewhere I need to be.'

She dropped the blouse she was unpinning, 'But you've only just got here, Love, you said you could stay until tomorrow.'

Alex brushed his jumper some more, 'Let her go, Sweetheart, she's in the ATS now, ain't you, Love. A very important person.'

Mum took my hands, 'But, Lily, don't go, what's happened? I've been looking forward so much to seeing you. Please don't go. Did you two have a row or something?'

I couldn't bring myself to tell a lie, so I said nothing. I took her hand. 'Why don't you walk with me to the station, Mum, just you and me.'

Alex's headed lifted, 'Can't let my two girls go all that way unescorted, can I? I'll come with you, one on each arm.'

I turned to look at him. 'No!' I said, venom making my voice harsh, 'You will not walk with us. I will walk with my mother, just my mother. Got it?'

He looked from me to her and back at me, then shrugged his shoulders. 'Your loss, Miss hoity-toity.' he said, heading back into the kitchen.

Mum unpegged the last few bits. 'What is it, love? You were a bit rude then. Not like you at all. What's got into you?'

My shoulders sagged at the thought of telling her. 'I'll explain as we walk mum, come on, get your umbrella.'

'It's true mum, that's what he said, I swear.'

My face scarlet, I'd just recounted the conversation with Alex, and mum had stopped dead in the street like she was turned to salt. I could hardly bring myself to repeat the intimate things he'd said about them, but forced myself because I hoped it would convince her I was telling the truth.

She stopped and turned towards me, 'I don't believe you. He'd never say such a thing,' she said, a quiver in her voice, 'he wouldn't.'

I took her hand, 'Why would I lie, Mum?'

She snatched it away, 'Perhaps you don't want me to be happy. Or you want me all to yourself. I don't know.'

I could hardly breathe, I was so upset. 'Mum, I promise you it's true and I want nothing more than for you to be happy.'

'How can I believe that when you haven't even bothered to get in touch with me for so long.' She was breathing fast and hard.

'I wrote three times. Didn't you get the letters?'

'I got one. One. That's all I'm worth. You must have had some leave. Why didn't you come home? Life more exciting somewhere else?'

'I couldn't, I was in...'

'Where? Where were you?'

I bit my tongue. 'I can't say. I wish I could, but it was somewhere where I couldn't get home for leave. But I can tell you it wasn't in this country.'

She stamped her foot. 'I don't recognise you any more. You're not the Lily who left here to join up. If this is what the ATS does to everyone, heaven help us.'

And with that, she turned on her heel and marched back towards the house.

My heart sank as I stood and watched her walk away. What had that Alex done to her to make her believe that I'd say something like that to make her unhappy? It was like she'd been brainwashed or something.

Rain splashed on my umbrella as I stood for several minutes trying to calm down and get my thoughts in some sort of order.

Should I go after her. Would that help? But Alex would still be there, poisoning her mind. It might even make things worse and anyway, I'd be sure to lose my temper with him. He'd tell her that it was a sign I wasn't right in the head or something.

Perhaps a letter would be better, but what if he saw it? I wasn't even clear if he'd moved in with her or not.

Unable to make up my mind I went back in and tried to hug Mum but she turned away from me.

'I hope we can soon be friends again,' I said, picked up my rucksack and left. Sadness weighing my steps I walked towards the home of my future in-laws, Edward's parents, Mr & Mrs Halpern.

His mother, I couldn't think of her as a Mum, had never liked me. I'm from the Corporation estate and they live in the expensive private road nearby But the two worlds were like different planets. She'd got a dutiful wife all lined up for Edward when I met him. Not that he wanted to marry the girl, or even knew his mum's intentions at the time, but she blamed me for ruining her plans of a big society wedding and a nicely spoken daughter-in-law who would be a carbon copy of her.

I'd never be that, life had taught me I had to have a mind of my own.

Their front door was painted bottle green, freshly washed, the knocker and letter-box sparkling. I took a deep breath and knocked firmly, telling myself to stand up straight and not be intimidated by her posh voice and the way she looked down her nose at me.

She blinked several times when she saw me, 'Goodness, it's Lily, where ever did you spring from?' She made no attempt to invite me in.

'I've got forty eight hours leave before my next posting. In London. I wondered if you had any news from Edward.'

She raised an eyebrow, 'I doubt we've heard any more than you.' she sighed and stood aside, 'You'd better come in, I suppose.' she called back over her shoulder, 'darling, it's Miss Baker.'

'Who?' I heard him call from the living room.

'You know, Lily. Edward's girlfriend.'

We were still standing in the hall. He came through and smiled broadly. He had aged more than he should have in the months since I'd seen him and his hair, previously pepper and salt was now completely white. My heart went out to him for his worry. We both feared the worst about Edward. He reached out for my hands. 'Lily, my dear, it's so lovely to see you. Whatever are you both doing in the hall like this? Come through.' He turned to his wife, 'Darling, can you make us some tea?'

The thought of having to make small talk with Mrs Halpern was too much after the scene with Mum, 'No no, I can't stop, I've got to get back to London this evening. I just wondered if there was any news of Edward. I haven't heard anything.'

The corners of his mouth turned down, 'Neither have we, I'm afraid, and it's so terribly worrying. We pray for him every night. As far as we know he's still missing. But no news is good news they say.'

I took my leave as politely as I could and headed back to the station, my steps dragging all the way. No news of Edward and my mother not speaking to me. This wasn't the home-coming I'd been looking forward to. Bronwyn and I both had dream scenarios of what it would be like when we escaped the Nazis. A lot of the time we didn't really believe we ever would, but the dreams gave us energy to go on and took our minds off the possibility of capture and worse.

The journey back to London was endless. The train was an hour late and four times we stopped for no apparent reason. I had to stand all the way, squashed between sweaty smokers. When I stepped onto the platform even the smoky station air seemed fresh by comparison.

Wishing I knew where Bronwyn was spending the night, I headed for a small hostel I'd heard was safe for women. I got a bus there, so weary I could hardly put one foot in front of the other. I was shocked to see some bomb damage on the way in one area we passed. I'd heard about the bombing when we were in Paris, but seeing it was still a shock. People had erected Anderson shelters and all sorts of preparations had been made but nothing much had happened yet. It's like the war was far away.

'What happened there?' I asked the woman sitting next to me, indicating the bomb site.

'It's like this,' she said, 'we have had the odd bomb. Nothing much like, but a few people have died and more have been made homeless. Let's hope we never get any more. Makes me shudder to think about it, it does.'

Although the bombing wasn't severe, everything looked drab like someone had washed the colour out of the city. Windows were either taped up or boarded over. White lines were painted on lamp-posts, trees and roadsides so people could see where they were going in the blackout. Everyone scurried along, their gas masks bouncing on their sides, wanting to get home in case the air raid sirens started.

The hostel was a tall, narrow building, three stories high and windows either side of the front door. I walked in and there was no-one to report to in the reception area. It was painted a drab cream colour with some faded prints on the wall and a well worn carpet. I called 'hello' a few times, but no-one answered so I went further in and found the kitchen. Four girls were sitting round the table, drinking tea and talking about the dance they planned to go to that night.

'Excuse me,' I said, 'how can I get a room for a couple of nights?'

One of them jumped up. She was tall and very thin and wore bright red lipstick and a Rita Hayworth hair style. 'Oh dear, I'm sorry, I'm supposed to be covering reception. Come with me.'

Ten minutes later, I had a room. It was small. Just wide enough for a narrow single bed, a chair by the bed and a couple of hooks to hang clothes on. Like the reception area, it was drab cream and the only splash of colour was the faded red curtains. I collapsed on the bed in a heap and burst into tears. The tension of the journey from Paris and the awful row with Mum as well as getting the cold shoulder from Edward's mother overwhelmed me. I cried for fifteen minute non-stop, every time I thought I'd stop, another memory would force its way into my head and I'd start again.

Finally, I went into the bathroom, washed my face and then went to the kitchen. I was glad to find it empty. I made some tea and toast and sat in silence until I'd finished them. Then I went to bed and slept for ten straight hours.

Bronwyn and me met at Kensington underground like we'd arranged, with half an hour to spare before we had to go to the office to get our postings. As we walked, I told her about Mum and what her horrible boyfriend said. I didn't intend to, but it was like I couldn't keep it in any more.

She stopped in her tracks, 'Dirty old bugger!' she said, 'I hope you're not blaming yourself for any of that. Trust me, I've dealt with loads of blokes like him. Next thing he'd be trying to get you and your mum in bed with him together.'

She stopped when she saw the look on shock on my face. I'd never heard of anything like that.

'You're so innocent,' she said, play punching my arm, 'You did the right thing getting out as quick as you did. He's the sort of bloke who'd have an answer for everything. Nothing you can do 'til your mum sees sense anyway.'

It was exactly what I needed to hear and my tense body relaxed a bit, 'You're right. He's a dirty bugger!' Then I paused, 'But what am I going to do about Mum?'

She put her hand on my arm, 'No idea, Cariad. Why don't we get ourselves all set up with jobs and somewhere to live, then we'll think about it.'

I knew she was right, we had enough to be getting on with. One more day, then starting our new jobs whatever they might be. And heaven knows if we'd be able to find somewhere to live in that time.

The office was in a very grand government building, pale stone with big double doors. I surprised myself by feeling scared to go in. I thought about all the things that had happened to me since I joined up would have made me tougher.

Bronwyn saw my fear. 'Come on, you daft ha'peth,' she said, pushing me forward, 'we'll be fine, they need us, and urgently if we only get two rotten days off.'

There was a grand entrance with stairs each side. Sounds echoed off the walls. It smelled of furniture polish and money. We climbed three sets of stairs to get to the right room number.

'Well, this is posh,' Bronwyn said, breathless from the climb, 'let's hope they're friendly people in there.'

We knocked on the door three times before someone called 'Enter.' It was a biggish room, enough space for four desks. Each desk had an in-tray piled high and a typewriter as well as the usual pens and pencils. On the wall behind the desks were metal shelves full of ring binders.

One woman looked up as we walked in, 'Yes?' she said, as if we'd interrupted her doing something important.

I took a deep breath, 'We were told to report at eleven o'clock to get our next postings.'

She looked us up and down, 'And why, may I ask, aren't you in uniform? This is most irregular.'

'It's like this, see,' started Bronwyn, 'we were in Paris and had to escape. We lost our uniforms and haven't been issued with new ones yet.'

The woman raised an eyebrow and her top lip curled, 'Oh, yes?'

It was too much. I stepped forward and put my hands on her desk, leaning forward so much she pushed her chair back.

'Yes. That's exactly what happened. While you've been sitting here in your comfortable office, we've been finding German spies in Paris, and running across the country trying to avoid capture. Then we got on one of the last ships back from Cherbourg, helping tend to injured soldiers. Anything else you want to say, or are you going to start being helpful and give us our postings?'

'Hear, hear!' Bronwyn murmured beside me, clapping her hands.

The woman's face was a mask. She stood up and realised her colleagues on the other desks had stopped working and were watching us all. When she looked at them, they looked quickly away and went back to what they were doing.

Without a word, she brushed past us and walked out the door slamming it behind her.

It was as if the whole room froze. No-one moved. Then a younger woman at the next desk stood up and came over to us. 'It sounds as if you've had a difficult time, girls. Let me help you.'

Twenty minutes later we were back outside, blinking in the daylight.

'Well, you're okay,' I said, 'Despatch rider! You never told me you could ride a motorbike.'

'With all the brothers I've got one or other of them was always terrorising the street riding up and down on some stolen bike.'

My jaw dropped, 'Didn't they ever get nicked?'

She gave a hollow laugh, 'Nah, our area was so rough, it was a no-go area for the cops. They never came near us unless there was an actual murder. And they only happened about once a year. If they lost one of the bikes it was 'cos the silly buggers rode it too fast out of our patch and got nabbed by the law.'

My jaw dropped further. This was making my childhood seem easy.

'It's like this, see,' she went on, ''cos they stole so many, I got to ride on different bikes, never for long mind. They were always clapped out old bangers. They used to dump them when they got bored. But it was good practice. I'm dead chuffed to be a despatch rider. Out on the open road.'

'All weathers.' I interrupted.

'I come from Wales, a bit of rain is nothing to me. It's the freedom I'm going to enjoy.'

We started to walk towards the underground station. 'What do you mean, freedom? You'll surely have deadlines, times when you're supposed to drop off messages or whatever it is.'

She nodded, 'That's true enough, but there'll be no-one breathing down my neck. I can choose which way I go to places and I'm not a bad map reader.'

'You're lucky then, my posting sounds dead boring. Office work in an Army depot. I thought they wanted us because we'd been biligual telephonists. Doesn't sound like either of us will do using our French much.'

A loud hooting from a passing car made us jump. Two lads wound down the car window, 'Want a lift, sexy ladies?' they called, blowing kisses and making rude gestures.

'Do you use that dirty mouth to kiss your mother?' Bronwyn shouted at them, then turned back to me. 'Stupid lads. Who'd want idiots like that? I'm going to find me someone more mature, an older man whose got a bit of money and knows how to treat a girl right.'

'Well, I suppose you'll meet loads of people if you're a despatch rider...'

'And we can go to clubs and things now we're in London. You still hopeful about Edward?'

We crossed the road, dodging cars and horse droppings, 'Of course, though truthfully I can hardly remember what he looks like. It seems like it was another life when I met him, what with all we've been though.'

We stopped in a little greasy spoon cafe and thought about where we should look for somewhere to live. The depot I was going to work in wasn't too far away from where Bronwyn would be based. We looked at an underground map and wondered where we could afford.

A bloke at the next table leaned over. He still had his flat cap on and a ciggie hanging out of the corner of his mouth.

'Hope you don't mind, girls, but I overheard your conversation. If you need a cheap area, you'd better look around *here* and *here*.' He stabbed his finger at the map, 'It'll be rough though, nothing fancy, but you might find something you can afford.'

I smiled at him, 'We only need a couple of rooms. But thanks for the suggestion, we'll try there. It's got an underground station.'

'And there's plenty of buses too.' he said, 'why don't you ask at the station there? Someone might have some ideas. You'll need luck. With bombings rooms are getting harder to find.'

We stood up, 'Now, we need to get cracking finding somewhere to live or I'll be joining you in the hostel tonight.' Bronwyn said, tugging at my arm.

~

The landlord stood in the doorway of the rooms, a cigarette hanging out of his mouth, 'You going' in or what?' he said, and ash from the cigarette dropped on his beer-stained shirt. We took a couple of steps forward.

'I don't...' I started.

Bronwyn spun on her heel, 'We don't need to go any further.' She stepped towards the landlord. Anyone else might have felt threatened by her jutting chin and firm step, but he just looked at her with dead eyes.

'What do you think girls, all right for you? May be able to come sort of arrangement about the rent, know what I mean?' He gave a crude wink.

Bronwyn pushed past him, indicating for me to follow. 'This place is only fit for rats,' she said, 'and there are plenty already at home here. You should be ashamed.'

He just shrugged, closed the door and locked it. We were already half way down the stairs, 'Your loss! Stuck up cows!' he shouted after us.

Outside, we took a deep breath, relieved to be away from the smell of filth, cooking and rot.

'Come on, let's look for somewhere else before we get too downhearted.' I said.

We'd already knocked on a dozen doors. Quite a few of them had signs saying 'No blacks, Irish or dogs.' Most of the landlords or landladies took one look at us and said the rooms were already gone.

'A lot of people forget to take their signs down, don't they?' I said after the third time it happened.

Bronwyn stopped in her tracks, 'It's because of me. Didn't you realise?'

I frowned, 'What on earth do you mean. Why should it be because of you?'

She put her hands to her face, 'Look at this. I'm not exactly white, am I?'

'But you're not black.'

She gave a bitter laugh, 'Depends on your point of view. Not exactly an English Rose am I? I'm used to it. Swansea's full of people like me, half and half, but that doesn't stop the white people being down on us all the time. I'm telling you the truth now, school was terrible, always being called names. Nig-nog, blackie, monkey face and loads of others. Lucky there was a few of us and we did our best to stop anyone trying to beat any of us up. And my brothers were big lads. They'd go after anyone who upset me.'

By now we came to another big house that had a 'rooms to let' sign outside. There was no sign saying no blacks, Irish or dogs. The door was opened by an elderly lady, so thin her wrap-around pinny could have gone round her twice. Her hair was thinning and her cheeks were hollowed out.

We explained we wanted to look at the rooms, 'Well, come in my dears,' she said and I could feel the tension draining away. I hoped the rooms would be as nice as her. 'It's up on the second floor,' she said leading the way, 'this place belongs to my son, but he's away fighting, so I'm looking after it for him. I live here.' She nodded at a door on the ground floor.

We followed her upstairs, walking slowly as she grumbled about her painful knees. 'Two sets of rooms each floor plus a bathroom,' she said, 'if you take the rooms you'll have to be quick in the morning to get any hot water though.'

She stopped and took a key out of her pocket, 'Here, these are the rooms.'

We stepped inside. The first room doubled up as a kitchen with a tiny sink and a gas ring in a little alcove curtained off. There was an old metal fireplace with a grate. The walls were a bit grubby but nothing that a good wipe wouldn't sort out. The furniture had seen better days, and was stained here and there. There was a settee, and armchair, a wonky side table and a small wooden table and two chairs. Bronwyn went over the settee and poked it about, 'No flees.' she said with a smile.

'Bedroom's through there, ducks.' the old lady said, opening the door so we could see.

The room was just big enough for two narrow single beds, a double wardrobe and a wooden chair. Bronwyn sat on the beds and bounced a bit, 'Seems okay,' she muttered, then went over to the window.

'Go on, open it up,' the old lady said, 'bit of flat roof out there. You can climb out and sit there on a nice day. One or two tenants in the past had a few plant pots out there. Flowers and things, very pretty.'

It wasn't much of a view, a brick wall one side that might make it a sun trap, then the sides or fronts of other buildings. As we leaned out Bronwyn looked at me and I nodded.

We turned back, 'How much did you say it was?' I asked.

We could just about afford it. 'Can we move in straight away?' I asked, 'we're in the ATS and just been posted here. Got to start our new postings tomorrow.'

'That'll be okay, but we've got some rules. Don't like having them, but got to protect all the other people living here.'

The rules were on a notice on the back of the door:

No visitors after 10pm

No loud music

No pets

No longer than ten minutes in the bathroom

Don't use all the hot water

Keep your rooms clean

. . .

'I clean the stairs and bathrooms,' she said when we'd finished agreeing to the rules, 'But that don't mean you can be slobs. I expect everyone to clear up after themselves. Don't leave your stuff in the bathroom, or your shoes on the landing either.'

Two hours later, we were back and unpacked our few things. We made some tea and went to sit on the flat roof.

It was late afternoon, and the temperature was dropping. We grabbed a blanket each off our bed and wrapped them round our shoulders.

'Don't know about them rules,' Bronwyn said, pointing to the list on the back of the door, 'do you think we'll need a list too. We never shared a room in Paris, did we?'

A heaviness weighed down my chest when I remembered how my room-mate met her end. She'd been caught as a German spy and killed herself rather than go to prison. I bit my lip, 'Well, I know you're not as tidy as Ingrid was but I expect we'll manage. Let's agree to tell each other if we're getting fed up with something.'

'Working in a depot sounds boring,' Bronwyn said, probably trying to take my mind off Ingrid who we'd both liked, 'tell you the truth, I think I've got the better posting.'

I took a sip of my tea, 'You're not kidding. Do you think you'll only be riding round London?'

She shrugged, 'No idea. It's be good to get out of the city sometimes. I suppose we'll both know more tomorrow. I'll have to get some warm clothes though. We had to leave most of us stuff behind in Paris, didn't we. Get some Long Johns to go under my uniform.'

I thought about the meagre amount of money we'd been given two days ago. It wouldn't stretch to buying clothes.

'First payday, we can go to the market and see what we can find. Wonder if there's any jumble sales coming up soon?'

'Leave your bag there and I'll show you around the depot.' Mr McDonald was my new boss and keen to get me started, 'We've been asking for someone for ages. Important work we do here, keeping the military stocked with everything they need.'

We headed out of the office building and into the yard. The yard was so big it was difficult to see it all in one glance, and much of it was covered in buildings or lorries moving here and there. It was more or less square. One side was bordered by the road where I'd come from on a number 57 bus. The opposite side was bordered by a railway line, a third by houses and the other couldn't be seen because of one of the two massive warehouses.

Men were everywhere, loading or unloading lorries; pushing trollies stacked with goods from one place to another, or painting the side of one of the warehouses. Between the road, the railway and all the activity it was a noisy place and smelled of petrol fumes and smoke from the trains. Dust swirled like miniature whirlwinds here and there, lit by the morning sun.

'Let me show you what's what.' Mr McDonald said, leading me to the nearest warehouse. He had a funny side-to-side walk, probably caused by his very fat legs or arthritic hips. The noise inside the warehouse was deafening, but what struck me most was how organised it all was. Floor to ceiling shelves were loaded with an enormous variety of things, all clearly labelled. He saw my look of surprise.

'People don't think about it, but we have to supply everything from guns to food.'

'But surely the cooks must buy fresh food locally.'

He nodded, 'They do, you're right, but we have the canned and bottled stuff. Even with everyone Digging for Victory and turning their flower gardens into vegetable plots, there's not enough food to feed the whole population. There are warehouses all over London and the country, this is just one of many. Did you notice the guards as you came in?'

I shook my head. I'd been so busy looking for where I had to report, I hadn't seen them at all.

'We have to guard against stuff going missing. Everything is checked in and checked out.' He stopped and took me out of the warehouse to an area where we wouldn't be overheard. 'I was told you'd uncovered a German spy while you were in Paris. That's one of the reasons I particularly wanted you. You must be good at keeping your eyes open.'

I had no idea that sort of information would be passed on and felt embarrassed. 'Is that what you want me to do then?'

He waved his arm to indicate the whole yard, 'You won't be responsible for that on your own. Like I said, we check everything in and out, but the more people on the alert the better. You'll be doing some typing and switchboard work, but I'm going to make sure you sometimes have to come out in the yard.'

I swallowed hard, 'But what if I don't find anything?'

'No-one's going to blame you. Just keep your eyes and ears open, that's all I ask. Report to me if you're suspicious about anything. Come on, let's get inside and I'll show you where you'll sit. You'll find some of the girls here are soldiers like you and some are civilians.'

My desk was in a small room with three other girls who all stopped typing and looked up when I walked in. Two smiled and said hello; the third ignored me and went back to what she was doing.

Mr McDonald coughed loudly, 'Can I introduce you to Lily Baker,' he said, 'she'll be working with you. Normally she'd be in uniform, but she needs a few days to sort that out. She can type and do switchboard work. I hope I can count on you all to take her under your wing and make her feel at home.'

He pushed me forward. The girl nearest stood up and leaned over her typewriter. 'I'm Edith, pleased to meet you.' She was a wispy sort of girl, her uniform hung off her and she was pale and looked underfed. But her smile was friendly and I was relieved I'd be sitting next to her.

She looked at the girl next to her, 'This is Marion.' she said. Marion moved forward and shook my hand, 'Nice to meet you, you'll soon find your way round.' she said. She was plump with rosy cheeks and thick brown wavy hair.

The third person finally looked up. She was older, perhaps mid forties. Deep frown lines etched her forehead and her mouth naturally turned down at the corners. She was not in uniform. 'I'm Mrs Blake, and I'm your supervisor,' she finally said, 'you come to me if you've got any problems with your work. No need to bother Mr McDonald.'

I hoped I wouldn't need to turn to her for help very often.

'Now, I'll leave you to it,' Mr McDonald said, 'Mrs Blake will give you your work each day. Come to see me before you go this evening and let me know how you get on.'

'Come and sit here,' Edith said, patting the desk next to hers. I took off my coat and sat looking at the scratched wooden desk top. The typewriter and wire basket were the only things on it. A chair scraped on the floor and Mrs Blake came towards me with a pile of papers. 'Type these reports, one carbon copy, no mistakes.' she said, thrusting them into the wire basket. 'Tippex and a rubber in the drawer. Ask me if you can't read any of the handwriting, don't guess and waste paper, there's a war on. Paper and other things you'll need are in the stationary cupboard over there.'

'But what about switchboard work?' I asked.

'No need to worry about that. It's only in an emergency if two girls are off. If that happens they'll give you the training.'

'I'm used to using a switchboard.'

'Well, let's hope it's the same type then.'

For most of the day the only sound in the room was the thumping of the typewriter keys or the sound of paper being rolled in or pulled out. But each time Mrs Blake left the room, the atmosphere changed completely and Edith and Marion came to life.

'You got a bloke?' Edith asked, looking at my engagement ring.

My body felt cold, 'I have, I'm engaged. But Edward is listed missing, has been for several months. He's with the Royal Berkshire Regiment.'

'And you've heard nothing?' Marion asked, 'Still, I suppose no news is good news and all that. Edith's husband is missing, too.'

I turned to Edith, it was the first time I'd come across anyone in the same situation as me. 'How long is it since your husband went missing?'

She sighed, 'Six weeks. He was... is... a Flight Engineer and his plane went down over France but no-one saw it catch fire so I keep hoping he's okay. Maybe he parachuted out.'

'Lots of the boys parachuting over France get shot dead while they're still in the air.' Marion said, putting a new sheet of paper in her typewriter.

'Marion!' I said, unable to believe how insensitive her comment was.

Edith shook her head, her thin fair hair moving, 'Take no notice, Lily. You'll soon learn that when God made Marion he forgot to give her any tact. Did you get the letter about Edward then? Him going missing?'

I shook my head, 'No, we're not married so it would have gone to his mum. She never showed me.'

She reached into her bag and bought out a well-worn envelope, 'This is the letter I got. Do you want to read it? I expect your Edward's mum will have got a similar one. When my mother-in-law saw it she fainted clean away. I had to use smelling salts to bring her round. Banged her arm on the table she did as she fell, had a nasty bruise, poor thing. That was the least of our worries though.'

She handed me a sheet of paper that had been read so much the folds were almost falling apart.

'D*ear Mrs Robson,* (it said)

May I be allowed to express the sympathy of myself and the squadron with you concerning the sad news of your husband Sidney.

The aircraft in which he was flying took off to attack a target near Paris and nothing further has been heard although some witnesses say they saw the plane descend, but not catch fire. These comments have not been verified.

You may be aware that in quite a large percentage of cases missing aircrew are eventually reported prison of war, and I hope this may give you some comfort.

Your husband was a most proficient Flight Engineer and well-liked by his colleagues. His loss is deeply regretted by us all.

We need to explain that we do not have any further information at this time. Once again, please accept the deepest sympathy of us all, and let us hope we may soon have some good news about the safety of your husband.'

Yours sincerely,

Wing Commander D.F. Smyth

I handed the letter back to Edith, 'It must be hard to know what to think after reading that.'

'That's right, it reads in some places like they know he's dead, then in others like he might still be alive. I go from despair to hope every day. Two days after we got the letter I was walking down the road and a bloke in uniform just like him walked towards me, a long way down the road though. I thought it was him and it was like my heart jumped and I started to run towards him. Then I realised it wasn't him at all and burst into tears. I felt such a fool.'

I reached over and put my hand on her arm, 'Poor you, that must have been awful. Do you know how much effort they put into finding missing soldiers and airmen?'

She shook her head, the corners of her mouth turned down. 'No idea. They don't tell you anything but the bare facts, do they. Me and his mum have been beside ourselves wondering if he's still alive.'

'Do you get on well with her, then?'

Her eyes sparkled, 'Yes, she's lovely is Joan. My mum died when I was a kid and she's been like a second mother to me. I've known her for ever. What about your Edward's mum? Do you get on with her?'

My heart felt weighed down just thinking about Mrs Halpern. 'No, she thinks I'm not good enough for Edward, barely speaks to me.'

We would have said more but just then Mrs Blake came in and we all pretended we'd been working non-stop.

I'd been in my new posting for a week when the phoney war ended. Everywhere there were posters telling us what to do in the case of an attack, yet not many bombs had dropped. It was as if no-one knew what to believe. Was the government alarming people for nothing or should everyone really be scared and prepared? Hundreds of children had been evacuated from London and other big cities to the country. Some mothers had gone so far as to get them back because London felt safer than they'd been led to believe.

The air raid practices regularly had people running to their Anderson shelters or the underground stations, but as the weeks went by, fewer people bothered.

But then September the bombing started in earnest.

Bronwyn and I were sitting on the flat roof when the sirens went off. 'Shall we bother?' I said, tired of the endless rehearsals. We very soon got our answer.

We heard them first.

The sound of hundreds of bombers heading towards London. We'd already learned that often you couldn't really hear just one bomber, because they were so high, but when there was so many it was another matter. It took a few seconds to identify the noise, but then we couldn't get back inside quickly enough.

We grabbed a few things and dashed out of the door, competing for stair space with other people in the building who all looked as tense as we felt. The sky outside stopped us in our tracks. Hundreds, literally hundreds, of bombers were flying over us, all in formation. They seemed to blot out the sky. The sight made my insides turn to liquid and my knees shake. Before we'd gone ten yards toward the tube station that was our designated air raid shelter, we saw bombs dropping. 'That's the docks!' someone shouted near me.

Along with hundreds of other people we ran to the tube station and there was such a crush we had to queue to get in. Air Raid Wardens tried to keep some sort of order, shouting and blowing their whistles and helping people who couldn't walk well. You could feel the fear in the crowd. People pushed and shoved trying to get below ground. I took a final glance just before I took the stairs down and saw patches of terrifying red sky: loads of fires in different parts of the city. Nearer there were the white streaks of bullets from the anti-aircraft guns dancing like a deadly firework display. I heard the drone of one engine change and turned to see a Nazi plane heading towards its doom. I wanted to cheer, but then remember it would probably kill people when it fell to earth.

'Come on!' shouted Bronwyn, pushing me down the stairs, 'get a move on!'

The platform was already packed and people were claiming a space for themselves, sometimes keeping one free for loved ones yet to appear. Some were prepared and had blankets, sandwiches and flasks of tea. Like people on an underground train, they spread themselves out but the gap between them soon filled up as more and more people joined the crowd. Carrying our kitbags, we stepped over people trying to find a space big enough for two. Most people were good natured if we trod on their blanket or their toes, but one or two rained curses on us.

We managed to find a space where we could sit with out backs to the wall and counted ourselves lucky. The platform was packed, but still people came down although it was only a trickle.

'Not being funny or nothing, but it's getting a big niffy in here.' Bronwyn said, as someone let out a loud fart, 'suppose it'll be worse before we're done.'

We looked around at the mixture of people. Most looked ordinary, not rich or very poor, but here and there we could see a couple or sometimes a family who were dressed in clothes that cost a lot. 'Wonder what they're doing here.' I murmured, 'surely they'd have their own shelter?'

Bronwyn looked over to where I indicated, 'Probably out having a meal or something and couldn't get home in time. Strikes me these places will make people who never usually see each other all have to put up with it together.'

Despite being well under ground, we could faintly hear the crump of bombs dropping. At first, we looked nervously up at the sound, but gradually learned to ignore them as best we could. All around us we could hear snatches of conversation about the bombing, *'I wonder if Jim will be safe?' 'Will we still have a house to live in when we go back up?' 'How much longer can this go on?' 'Our Father, who art is heaven...'*

Then a man near us got out a mouth organ and started to play a sad tune. 'For God's sake, let's have something more cheerful.' someone shouted. The musician promptly stopped then starting playing *A-Cent-Tchu-Ate the Positive*. I nudged Bronwyn and we started to sing along with him. Someone else joined in and within half a minute there were at least half the crowd singing. It certainly helped us to eliminate the negative like the song said. When he'd finished, people shouted requests and for a good twenty minutes we forgot the awful things going on over our heads and enjoyed a sing-song. Nothing ever sounded so good.

About an hour later, people started to settle down for the night, laying squashed as sardines in a tin. A fair few even lay on the railway line in between the metal tracks. Then, without warning, a crump sounded very loud and the ground shook. Dust and plaster drifted down from the ceiling and a few people screamed. The sound of prayers got louder. I hardly dared breathe. When the loud bombing noise wasn't repeated, the tension on the platform slowly lessened although we could hear people sobbing here and there.

Bronwyn and I wrapped our thin blankets round ourselves, leaned against each other and tried to sleep.

'Thank goodness it's Sunday tomorrow,' I said, 'Doesn't matter if we don't get much sleep.'

Fear and being uncomfortable made my sleep fitful. My dreams were a muddle of bombs dropping, Edward proposing, then horribly, Edward dead in a field. When I woke up I was so tired it was like I'd never slept a minute. I was relieved when the all-clear sounded. Dreary from sleep, people gradually gathered their families and belongings around them and headed back towards the stairs.

The sight outside stole our breath. London was burning. Where before there were patches of fiery red, now the whole city seemed to be ablaze. An explosion a little way away made us all cower. 'What's that?' someone screamed. An ARP warden who was helping people to get back home shouted, 'It'll be a gas main or something. Not more bombs. Get along home now.' He blew his whistle and got people who'd been stopped in their tracks moving again. It was slow going. People were tired, fearful of what they'd find round the next corner. Some carried children or helped the elderly or infirm. Here and there fires still smouldered from the incendiary bombs and we could hear the sirens from the fire engines and ambulances as they rushed to help people and property. More ARP wardens were doing their best to put out the fires and many men in the crowd stopped to help them.

Wearily, Bronwyn and I turned the corner and stopped as suddenly as if we'd been hit in the face with a cricket bat.

Not two houses from our own, there was a gaping hole. The entire building was like it never existed. Instead there was just a smoking pile of rubble. 'Dear God, I hope they got out.' I prayed.

Two ARP men were searching through what was left of someone's home. We ran over. 'Can we help?' I asked the nearest man. His face was lit pink from the glow in the sky. He looked as if he hadn't slept for a month and there were dirty streaks across his cheeks. He turned to look at me, 'I've looked at my list and we don't think there's anyone in here, but we're not sure. Help us listen in case anyone's calling.'

It was a difficult task. There was so much noise around us with people calling for each other, the sound of incendiary bombs being put out, bricks falling here and there, all against the background sound of a city on fire.

I turned back to the man, 'Do you know who lives here?'

He nodded and got out a folder. Turning the pages he ran his finger down each line. 'Four people, it says here. Two live upstairs, and two down. Oh, and three children. We'll start digging, but keep your fingers crossed they come back any minute. They're probably in one of the shelters.'

We put down our kitbags and helped move bricks, bits of broken furniture and the sad remnants of people's lives out of the way. We couldn't hear anyone calling. Then our prayers were answered and the two families came running up. They were safe and sound, but homeless. They stood looking at the remains of their homes speechless with shock, and one of the children started to cry. A third ARP warden went over to them, and I noticed for the first time it was a woman. She stood in front of them and spoke gently, 'This is too much to deal with now. Go to Green Street school. They are prepared for people who've been made homeless.' They looked at her but it was clear they couldn't take in what she was saying.

She gently nudged them in the right direction, 'That's it, Green Street school. Go there now.' She was stopped by the low keening of one of the women, who was in a state of collapse. She was heavily pregnant and I noticed her feet and ankles were very swollen. Her husband had his arm round her back, keeping her from falling on the ground. Bronwyn looked at me and we nodded to each other. We picked up our kitbags and headed towards to sad group, 'Come on, we'll take you there.' She went in front and I walked behind, making sure they stayed together. It was only a few streets away but took ages. The pregnant woman kept stopping and clutching her stomach and we wondered if she was beginning to go into labour.

'I hope there's a doctor at that school.' Bronwyn said.

I nodded, 'Mind you, my experience is every street has someone who knows how to deliver a baby. Let's hope it's all straightforward.'

We carried on although walking was difficult because of the emergency vehicles and debris from the bombing. Once we'd got the group safely to the school, we went back to our rooms and collapsed on our beds without stopping to get undressed.

My last thought as I drifted into sleep was that I would become an ARP warden.

I t took me three times longer than usual to get to work next day. The buses kept making detours because of bomb damage to the roads and piles of bricks that still had to be moved out of the way. Buildings were still smouldering and here and there we could see people desperately scrabbling through the remains of their home searching for their belongings.

'Some of them'll be looters.' a man sitting near me said.

I turned to him, 'What, people will steal from a bombed house? That's wicked.'

'Can be.'

I frowned, 'What do you mean, can be? It's got to be.'

He shrugged, 'It's true a lot of the looters are crooks. You wait, you'll see them selling stuff they've nicked on the markets. But I remember what happened in the last war. Sometimes people walked past a bombed house and see something of no particular value. A book or a pencil, say, and just help themselves. Couldn't call them criminals, could you? Especially if everyone who lived there was dead or moved somewhere else. Desperate times make law-abiding people do things they wouldn't normally do. Couldn't hang them for that.'

For the rest of the journey I was silent, thinking about what he'd said. The government had laws about looting and it was punishable by hanging. Would you really hang someone for stealing a pencil?

~

Even miserable Mrs Blake joined in the conversation about the bombing, although she complained about me being late. On my way in, I'd noticed fewer men in the yard than normal, so I guessed other people were having trouble getting in on time.

True to his word, Mr McDonald had been giving me tasks that would take me to the yard most days. I'd kept my ears and eyes open as he said, but hadn't noticed anything amiss.

But the day after the bombing I caught a snatch of a conversation between two of the men, 'Got a good radio from one of the bombed houses.' he said. I pretended to get a stone out of my shoe so I could stay and listen but they spotted me and walked off. I walked over to one of the supervisors and asked the man's name. 'Frank Tyler,' he told me. It wasn't proof that he was up to anything shady in the yard, but I reported it to Mr McDonald anyway. It showed the man didn't have many scruples. Or did it?

Every day I asked Edith if there was any news of her husband, but the answer was always the same.

'Is there anything we can do to find out more?' I asked. Neither of us knew where to start but I decided to ask around. Someone must know.

When I saw Bronwyn I told her about reporting the man who'd stolen a radio. 'Does this make me a snitch?' I asked. It was several days later. She often came in late and left early, or more often I was in the shelter and we didn't see each other.

She thought for a minute, 'Sort of, I suppose. But what if he nicked stuff that got into the wrong hands? Say he stole a gun and it got back to a Nazi sympathiser? Or he stole food so the soldiers went short. No, you did the right thing. Mind you, if you had a pair of stockings going free I wouldn't say no.'

We sat and listened to the news. The BBC tried to make things seem not too bad, but we couldn't believe it. The bombers had been over every single night for the last week and there was no way of knowing when they'd stop. Maybe they'd flatten the whole of London. Every night the city burned and the mornings were full of anguish and the smell of burning and death.

'You still thinking of joining the ARP lot?' Bronwyn asked when we turned off the radio.

I nodded, 'Yes, I'm signing up tomorrow. The depot is as boring as you said it'd be and it doesn't really feel like I'm doing my bit for the war effort there.'

She pulled a face, 'Rather you than me doing ARP work. I'm making the most of all this.' She waved her arm around as if to indicate *everything*.

I turned to her, 'What do you mean, making the most of it? Is that why you've been home so late? I thought you were working.'

'Sometimes I am, but Henry is worth staying out late for. He's very kind.'

'Who's Henry? You've never mentioned him before. Is he someone you work with?'

She tapped the side of her nose, 'Ask no questions...'

She opened her bag and took out a bracelet. I took it from her and whistled, 'This looks expensive. What did you have to do for it?'

She winked, 'Nothing a lot of people aren't doing. We could all be dead tomorrow. Live while we can, get the most out of each day, that's my motto.'

My words caught in my throat, 'You mean you're...'

Her grin stretched from ear to ear, 'Oh, come on. Who's not?' She paused and looked at me, 'Oh, you I suppose, waiting for Edward like the good girl you are. What if we got bombed tomorrow? Do you want to die without ever having done it?'

My mind went blank. I'd always been bought up to believe you had to be married before you went with a man. Girls who didn't got into trouble and were rejected by their families and had to go away to have their babies adopted. Or they were called a slut or the village bike, and no decent boys would look at them. But I knew what Bronwyn was saying was true. I'd heard enough comments at work to know that traditional values were changing, people were doing things they wouldn't have done before the war.

'Who is this Henry anyway?' I asked.

She looked down at the bracelet, turning it round and round. 'He's an officer, I told you. One of the good ones.'

Her cheeks went pink, and I narrowed my eyes, 'Bronwyn, is he married? Tell me you're not going out with a married man.'

Her back straightened. 'What of it? His wife is over two hundred miles away. They haven't had sex for...'

'Oh, Bronwyn, surely you don't believe all that. You'll be saying she doesn't understand him next.'

'She doesn't. She...' she went silent, then jutted out her jaw, 'Anyway, what she doesn't know can't hurt her. It's not like he's in love with me and going to leave her. We're just having a bit of fun. We only see each other once a week or fortnight. It looks like I'll be going to Maidenhead regularly and have to stay over. Tell you the truth, I think I'll look out for little romance there too. Could save on the cost of a room for the night and have someone to keep me warm.'

My jaw dropped open, 'You mean you'd have two of them at the same time?'

She laughed, 'Well, not in the same bed at the same time. Not even in the same town, but where's the harm? Tell me that.'

I thought about it that night in bed. What she was doing felt wrong, but did it really do anyone any harm? And if it didn't how could it be wrong? I didn't know what to think.

With bombing happening every night, the government was desperate for more Air Raid Precaution volunteers. So only a week after I enquired about joining up, I started my classes. I'd seen ARP wardens with their tin hats with a big W on the front many times. I knew they helped get people to air raid shelters and make sure everyone observed the blackout. I hadn't realised they were responsible for handing out gas masks and pre-fabricated air-raid shelters.

I was glad to find my ATS training meant I had more of the skills we needed than some other people. But there was still a lot to learn. To practice skills like first-aid and rescue, we were divided into groups. As far as they could, we were with people who would be working near us. I was with a man called David and a women called Edna. I was ashamed to notice that David was very attractive. He had hazel-brown eyes and thick brown hair that fell over his forehead. With a dimple that would put many film-stars to shame I could hardly take my eyes off him. I guessed he was probably five years older than me and he had no wedding ring on. But I noticed a ridge on his third finger and guessed he'd been married. I wondered what happened to his wife or if he just took off his ring when she wasn't around to see.

Edna noticed him too. I kept seeing her glancing his way. She was an older woman, painfully thin, her face gaunt. She had a wonderful sense of humour though and we laughed frequently as we dropped 'patients' on the floor or messed up bandages. Once when we had to bandage a broken arm, she spotted that the 'bone' sticking out of it was lamb bone and made to put it in her bag for her dog. We had to wrestle it off her.

'Glad I've still got Rover,' she said after she made us

promise she could take the bone home at the end of the evening, 'Glad I didn't take any notice of that rotten government telling us all to kill our pets.'

I was puzzled, 'What do you mean? I didn't hear about that.'

She frowned, 'Where you been, girl? It was in all the papers. Get your pets out to the country or put them down, that's what the top brass was saying. I heard say that three quarters of a million poor cats and dogs got the chop in a week. Whatever did they do with all the bodies, that's what I'd like to know.'

I was astounded. Three quarters of a million pets. It must have all happened when I was in Paris, but I couldn't tell her that.

'A lot of people must be missing their pets a lot.' I said.

She nodded and wrapped a bandage round the bone. 'You're not kidding. Two of my elderly neighbours are lost without their dogs to talk to, really lonely, widows from the Great War both of them. And they don't go out as much as they used to now there's no need to walk their dogs. I keep telling them to go out anyway, not good for them to keep sitting around.'

During the lessons, we learned about black-out regulations, working with emergency services to rescue people, helping people find their families after being made homeless and a whole load of other things. Although the thought of being out and about during the bombing was terrifying, I knew I'd be doing something useful, more useful than my work at the depot.

The depot job was proving as boring as I thought it would be, and I was glad of the variety the ARP training offered. The typing was very routine work and it was a relief to get out to the yard each day on my spying mission. Not that I spied much going on. After a while, I got the distinct impression the men were suspicious of me. They were polite and friendly, but they always kept their distance. Often, too, I'd see that they were spreading the word that I was about. I swear it was a particular whistle they did. After hearing it, I'd see someone suddenly put something away, or move to a different place. There was nothing I could be definite about though.

The girls I worked with were amazed I'd volunteered to be an ARP warden. Although plenty of women signed up, they still saw it as men's work and made cracks about me being power mad. Edith and I got quite friendly, drawn together by our missing men. Sometimes we'd go for a walk in our dinner break and dream about our futures as we ate our sandwiches.

'What sort of wedding do you want?' she asked as we walked down a side street trying to avoid the traffic and the bombed out houses.

I blinked hard, 'I... I... to be honest with you, I haven't thought about it.'

She gasped, 'You've been engaged for ages and not planned your wedding? Good heavens. Don't you want to get married? Is he a wrong 'un?'

I froze, and got angry with myself for not knowing how to reply. Did I want to get married? I realised for the first time that I had no idea.

Edith nudged me, 'Cat got your tongue?'

I rubbed the back of my neck, 'No, he's not a wrong 'un. He's a lovely bloke, kind and honest. It's not that. Trouble is, he's been gone so long I can hardly remember what he looked like.'

She stopped and looked at me, 'What then? If he's found

safe and sound you're going to have to make a decision one way or the other.'

I wished we'd never got into this conversation, 'It's just that I wonder if we'll still get on. His experiences are sure to have had an effect on him, and I know mine have. Will we still love each other? We've got to be different people after everything that's happened.'

She looked at her watch, 'Who knows? I suppose I'll be in the same boat if Sidney comes back after a long time. We'd better get back or we'll be late. Want to talk about it some other time?'

'Maybe. I need to think some more.'

She gave a little laugh, 'With all the things you do, I don't see how you ever get thinking time.'

Sometimes it seemed like Bronwyn didn't share rooms with me, I saw her so rarely. It might have been lonely, but most nights were spent either doing ARP work or in the shelter and there were always people to talk to. I didn't ask her again where she'd been each time we met. But I noticed new things on her side of the bedroom - a lipstick or some precious stockings or perfume. Once or twice I found a little gift for me, usually a bar of nice smelling soap.

So when she didn't come home one Saturday night, it was nothing out of the ordinary. Late afternoon Sunday there was a knock on the door, and I assumed she'd lost her key. But instead of her standing waiting to be let in, it was a man I'd never seen before. He had a battered brown suitcase at his feet. He was wearing a shiny suit and his tie was half undone. His trilby was at an angle, and a ciggie dangled from his lips.

'Bron in?' he said, looking me up and down.

I could feel my hackles rising, 'Bronwyn? No. Why do you want her?'

He shouldered past me, carrying the case, 'I'm Alun, her brother. I expect you've heard all about me.'

Without waiting to be invited, he sat himself down on the sofa, leaned back and stretched out his legs, crossing them at the ankles. I stood there for a moment not knowing what to say, breathless at his cheek. I put my hands on my hips, 'I've never heard of you. How do I know you're her brother? What are you doing here?'

He dug around in a pocket and produced his ration book. 'See? Alun Jones. That proves it.'

I laughed, 'Every other person in Wales in called Jones,' I said, 'That doesn't prove a thing.'

He wrinkled his nose, and opened his case. Searching through his things, he produced a photo taken at the seaside. 'See,' he said, thrusting it in front of my face, 'me and my sis at Mumbles beach. Satisfied now?'

I couldn't argue: it was Bronwyn all right, 'So what do you want?' I asked. I'd been bought up to be polite to visitors, but his rudeness made me act out of character.

'Somewhere to stay for a few nights, Bron'll be right made up to see me. And she never told me she shared with someone as lush as you though. Got a boyfriend?' he winked and took the cigarette out of his mouth, 'Got an ashtray, girl?'

I handed him a saucer, 'You can't stay here. There's only one bedroom and me and Bronwyn share it.'

He got up and walked over to our tiny kitchen corner. Without a word he put the kettle on, 'Fancy a cuppa? I make a good cup of tea, me.'

'No, and you can't stay here, there's no room.'

He leaned back against the sink, his hands in his pockets. 'Come on, don't be like that. It's only a few nights and Bron'll be tamping if you don't help her brother, like. The settee'll do me. Any road, it seems like we all have to sleep in the shelter every night.'

The kettle was beginning to hiss when there was another knock on the door. 'Bron forgot her key again?' Alun said as he spooned tea leaves into the pot, 'she was always doing that at home.'

But it wasn't Bronwyn, it was the landlady for her rent. As usual she had her money belt round her waist and her payment notebook at the ready. She was kindly but nosey, and stepped inside while I fetched her money. 'Gentleman caller I see,' she eyed Alun and folded her arms, 'you know gentlemen visitors have to be out by ten o'clock, don't you? Them's the rules.'

Alun stepped towards her, glancing at me, 'You didn't tell me you had such a charming landlady, Lil,' he said, his voice smooth as melted chocolate, 'I've never been that lucky anywhere I've lived.' My mouth dropped open as he took one of her hands and kissed it, then looked deep into her eyes. I wanted to gag, but to my surprise she went pink and stuttered, 'Well, I...'

Alun let go of her hand a little too slowly, 'I'm Alun, Bronwyn's brother, here all the way from Swansea. Very pleased to meet you. I hope you don't mind me saying that that's a very pretty cardigan you have on, it brings out the colour in your eyes.'

His smile would have melted an iceberg. If the iceberg had no brains at all. My landlady giggled, she actually giggled. Like a fifteen year old. 'I... nice to meet you Mr...?'

'Jones, but please call me Alun.' He took her hand again, 'I wonder if I could ask you a small favour, Mrs ...?

'Wheeler, Janice Wheeler.'

'Could I ask you a favour, Mrs Wheeler, Janice?'

She looked up at him, her lips slightly apart. 'What is it that you want?'

His smile reappeared, 'It's like this, see. I've just arrived from Swansea and I haven't got anywhere to live yet. I'm hoping you'll agree that I could stay here for a few days while I get myself sorted out. The settee would do me, and in any case I expect we'll be in the air raid shelter most nights the way things are going.'

A slight frown wrinkled her forehead, 'Are you working, Alun? Mr Jones?'

'Alun, please. I'm sorting out work starting tomorrow. I do a bit of buying and selling and I'll soon have something organised and get my own place. What do you think?'

He gave her a puppy dog look, all defenceless and big pleading eyes.

Mrs Wheeler wrung her hands, 'Well, this is very irregular, I don't usually allow such a thing to happen, but as it's you...'

He took her hand and kissed it again, 'Thank you so much, Mrs Wheeler, you won't regret it I promise you.'

I'd been watching all this like someone in a daze, unable to believe his behaviour. He deserved an Oscar.

'Here's your rent.' I said, breaking the moment. I got between them, and pressed the money into her hands, 'see you again next week.' I indicated she could leave, although she was a bit slow on the uptake. She gave Alun a final look as she finally left. He winked at her and blew her a kiss.

When the door was closed he raised one eyebrow, 'Silly cow, they fall for it every time. Killer with the ladies, me. Get them twisted round my little finger in no time.'

My eyes widened, 'Well, I can tell you it hasn't worked with me. I don't trust you any further than I could throw you.'

'Where's the tea strainer?' he asked, rooting around our meagre kitchen equipment. A minute later he turned and handed me a cup of tea, 'When you get to know me better, you'll feel different, see if I'm not right.'

He sat on the settee again and reached for another cigarette, 'Damn, that's my last one. I'll have to nip out for some more.'

I stood sipping my tea, waiting for him to leave. He took forever, smoking the ciggie down to the very end, his stained fingers showing this was a regular habit. Finally, he stubbed out the butt, slapped his knees and stood up. 'Right, more fags for me, see you later.'

'All the shops will be closed by now.' I said, noticing the time.

He tapped the side of his nose, 'Me, I can always find things I want. You'll learn.' He left his cup and saucer where it was and headed out the door. As soon as I heard his steps on the stairs, I flopped onto a chair and let out a deep breath. Although he hadn't been violent, my reaction to him reminded me of my dad and how me and Mum always had to be on guard when he was around.

I tidied and washed up the cups and saucers, then made myself a sandwich and a flask of tea in case the air raid sirens went yet again. I put them near the door with my book, torch and blanket. Then I sat looking out of the window, although with its criss-cross of brown tape the view was like a jigsaw puzzle. Would Bronwyn really want her brother staying with us? She'd never mentioned him, although she'd talked about having several brothers and sisters. But the way she spoke, it didn't seem as if she'd be bothered if she never saw any of them again. If only I knew when she was coming back, I could give her the responsibility of deciding what to do about him.

An hour later Alun still hadn't come back. If he hadn't left his case behind I'd have hoped he'd changed his mind. I settled down to read a book when the air raid siren went. I'd lost count of how many days in a row this was.

Grabbing my things, I hurried out of the door pulling it closed behind me. Only then did I realise I hadn't given Alun a key. But I had no intention of worrying about him. He'd surely be looking for somewhere safe too.

As I ran for the shelter, the streets were crowded again with people hurrying to get away from the destruction. The noise was like a blanket suffocating the brain, making rational thought slow and plodding. Anti-aircraft guns had begun to fight back at the German planes now and their shells lit the sky like fireworks again. But when the shells back down to earth, they could injure you badly, sometimes they killed people. We often took shelter from them as much as from the bombs.

Fear affected people differently. Some pushed others out of the way as they went to the shelters, not caring who got hurt in the process. Others helped children or elderly people, saying soothing words of encouragement that were drowned out by the sirens and the drone of the aircraft engines.

In the shelter I looked around for Alun but there was no sign of him. Bronwyn wasn't there either, but then I didn't expect her to be. I wondered if she was tucked up safe somewhere with her married lover, in a shelter somewhere on her own or out of London delivering important letters and packages on her motorcycle. Or even with another new man.

The woman next to me saw me looking around, 'Looking for someone special, love?' she asked.

'Just a friend, I expect she's in another shelter.'

She got a flask out of her bag, her hands gnarled with arthritis, 'You okay for tea, Sweetheart?'

I nodded, and got out my flask, 'Yes, thanks. You here on your own?'

She twisted her wedding ring round and round, 'Mmm, my Jim died a couple of years ago and my daughter's gone to stay with my brother in the countryside. Taken my grand-children with her. I miss them something rotten. But at least they're together, not split up like a lot of families.'

I put my hand on her arm, 'That's sad for you. Have you thought about joining them?'

'No, ducks, What'd I do in the country? I'm a Londoner through and through, can't stand all that fresh air. I'll wait this war out like I did the last one. What about you? I see you got an engagement ring on. Your young man away at war, is he?'

I nodded, 'Yes, but he's been reported missing so I have no idea if he's alive or not. It's like I can never relax because of the not knowing.'

She took a sip of her tea and licked her lips, 'Well, none of us know what's going to happen next day or next minute with all this damned bombing. What you doing about finding out more about what's happened to him?'

'Do?' I frowned, not sure what she meant, 'there's nothing I can do, is there? I have to wait until I hear more.'

She drained her cup, 'That was a nice cup of tea, but it never tastes as good out of a flask as it does at home, does it? No, what I mean is, have you thought about pestering the powers-that-be to see what they're doing to find him.'

'Can I? Who would I ask?'

She screwed the top back on her flask, 'No idea, ducks. I'd have to leave that to you to find out.'

It was one of those rare nights when I hadn't got anything on. It would have been good to have a quiet evening at home, but the air raid sirens put paid to that idea. I spend the evening trying to sleep in the underground station along with hundreds of other people. It was so uncomfortable, smelly and noisy I never slept for more than a few minutes at a time.

When I got home from the shelter, I was surprised to find Bronwyn there. I was relieved to see her safe and sound and gave her a spontaneous hug. Like all of us, she looked tired, dark rings round her eyes making her look older than usual.

'I'm so glad to see you.' I said, 'Have you been in the shelter? I couldn't see you.'

She hung up her leather coat, driving hat and goggles and fetched a glass of water, 'I have, but not the tube one. I was on my way back but I wasn't near enough. Some people in the next street let me squeeze in their Anderson shelter with them. Tell you the truth, they are horrible things, all damp and smelly.'

She gestured towards Alun's case, 'You moving out?' she asked with a grin.

I put the kettle on, then turned towards her. 'That case, it's your brother's. Alun's. Did you know he was coming?'

Her hand holding the glass of water stopped half way to her mouth, 'Alun's? My brother? He's here?'

I nodded, 'He came a few nights ago, said you'd be thrilled to see him and he wanted to stay.'

She sat down on the kitchen chair as if someone had kicked her legs from under her. 'But the landlady won't let us have anyone to stay.'

I pulled a face, 'He sweet-talked her. Had her eating out of his hand. You should have seen her, he turned her into a silly schoolgirl. She said he could stay a few nights. Mind you, I haven't seen him since. Goodness knows where he's been.'

Her hand went to her chest, 'Oh my goodness, what if he's been bombed and is dead or in hospital somewhere?'

'I don't think so, he comes when I'm at work. Leaves dirty dishes all over the place. Did you know he was coming?'

She snorted, 'Did I hell! I'd have told him to stay away. I know he's my brother and everything, but he's a bad 'un. Always up to mischief of some sort or another.'

I poured the boiling water in the pot, looking forward to a cuppa in a china cup, 'Well, then, if he comes back, shall we tell him to leave?'

She cleared her throat, 'I don't know, not being funny or nothing but it's awkward. It's not as if I love the blighter, but he is my brother. Can we give him a few days? Could you stand it?'

I was just about to agree when I spotted a package on the window cill. 'What's that then?' I asked.

She shook her head, 'Nothing to do with me. Go, on, open it.'

It was two pairs of stockings.

'What the... where did these come from?' I asked thin air.

She gave a bitter laugh. 'That'll be Alun. A peace offering. Goodness know where he's got them from. Tell you what though, I'm asking no questions. Come on, hand over one pair.'

I took my pair out of the packet and ran them through my fingers. They felt smooth as polished wood. I ran them across my cheek. 'These are bound to be black market,' I said, 'we shouldn't keep them.'

She looked at me as if I'd gone crazy, 'Oh come on, Miss Goody Shoes. Everyone has stuff on the black market. An egg here, a packet of ciggies there, it keeps us all sane. Just keep them and enjoy wearing them. Talking of that, any news of your Edward?'

I put the stockings back in the packet, resolving the keep them for a very special occasion. Drawing seams on the back of my leg with pencil would have to do til then. 'No, no news of Edward. I suppose no news is good news, but with so many men missing who knows if he's still alive or not.'

'Have you got a gut feeling about it?'

'No, not at all.' I wanted to change the subject. The truth was I did have a feeling and it wasn't good. Somehow I just knew he was dead. It was as if the very air I breathed changed one day. I could remember the day. It was several weeks earlier, a bright sunny day when you feel good to be alive. I was in the depot yard checking some things for the boss. But I was just walking along and it was like the sun went out and everything was darkness and gloom. My heart ached as surely as if someone had punched me in the chest and I found myself gasping for breath. One of the men in the yard saw me stumble and grabbed my arm before I fell over.

He looked closely at me, 'You alright, Miss? You look like you've just had bad news.'

I took a deep breath and gradually found I could think a bit more clearly. 'No, I'm okay, I just stumbled,' I said, giving him a half-hearted smile, 'thank you for stopping me from falling over.'

The feeling that Edward was gone had never left me. But I knew I couldn't necessarily trust it. Plenty of people had feelings about their love ones that turned out to be wrong. So there was no way I was going to tell anyone, not even Bronwyn. Every evening I said a prayer for his safety, but somehow I couldn't believe God was listening.

I turned my attention back to Bronwyn. 'What's happening with your love life? I'm really out of date with it.'

She stirred her tea and took a sip. It nearly burned her mouth. She poured some in the saucer and blew on it, then drank it straight from the saucer. 'That's lovely that is,' she said, 'well, you probably think I'm out with my man every night I'm not here, but it's nothing like that. Often I'm in another part of London or even further away when the sirens start and I have to shelter wherever I can. Often when the All Clear goes, it's not worth coming back here. I'd only get a little bit of sleep before I have to leave again.'

'What do you do then?' I had pictures of her sleeping on park benches.

'I go to the nearest shelter wherever I am. Or if I'm near the office I go to the medical room. Its got a couch for examinations, bit hard and not very comfortable but beggars can't be choosers and all that. I go in there and get a bit of shut-eye. No-one seems to mind.'

'But what about your bloke? Or it is blokes?' I tried to keep the disapproval out of my voice.

She took another sip of her tea, avoiding my eye. 'He's on the way out, I think. Haven't seen him much lately and he hasn't given me any presents for a while. I used to get them every time I saw him. Probably his wife's got wind of what's going on. Still, got my eye on someone else. Makes sense to have them lined up.' she looked at the clock and yawned. 'I'm too tired to think straight. Let's get to our beds.'

'No planes so far, we might be lucky. Jerry's probably bombing some other poor town.' David said. I was secretly thrilled that my first night on duty as an ARP warden was with David, the ARP warden I was attracted to. He'd already done three nights duty and I'd been paired with him so he could show me the ropes.

'Don't expect me to know everything about everything,' he warned, 'but I expect we'll muddle through between us.'

We spent an hour going round the streets in our patch making sure everyone was obeying the blackout.

A light showed through curtains in one house and we knocked on the door shouting, 'Put that light out!'

'Sod off, you bloody little Hitler!' was all the thanks we got for trying to save their lives.

'You'll get used to that,' David said, 'they all think we're puffed up Hitlers til they need us, then they change their tune.'

To be honest, the change from the gloom were almost a relief. It was a cool night with patchy cloud and so dark we could have been in the middle of the countryside, not in busy London. When the blackout was first introduced, I found my steps were hesitant as if I'd lost my sight. But gradually the blackness became charcoal and I sensed darker shapes in the black and listened to changes in background noise that indicated I'd come to a crossroads or a gap in the houses. And of course the shielded torches were a blessing. So were the white bands painted on trees and lamp posts.

If it wasn't for the sounds we could hear, we'd have thought the whole town was empty. But we could hear radios playing in the houses, the occasional sing-song, an argument or two and the footsteps of other people making their unsteady way home.

Then we heard a loud curse and the sound of someone falling. 'Where are you?' I called, 'Are you okay?'

A man's voice swore again, 'I'm okay, give me a minute to get up.'

We went over to him and the smell of booze was so strong it was unlikely he'd have noticed if a tram ran into him. 'Shorry,' slurring his words, 's'my birthday, had a little celebration.' he turned to me, 'Come on love, can't see you properly but I bet you're lovely. Give me a birthday kiss.'

'Not on your Nelly,' I said with a laugh, but gave him a little peck on the cheek. He turned to give me a hug, but I was quicker and managed to side-step him.

'Come on, let's get you home.' I said. He lived just a few doors along, so we escorted him to make sure he didn't fall over again. The door opened and his wife stood there, hands on hips. 'What time do you call this?' she hissed, 'We've all been waiting to have a knees up with you, you stupid bugger.' We turned and left them to it.

We hadn't gone further than another hundred yards when David stopped and held my arm, 'Listen!' he said. Half a minute later I heard it. 'That's a German plane.' he said,

I bit my lip, 'Really? How can you tell? I can't hear anything.'

'Listen hard,' he said, 'the engines aren't synchronised. British ones are. Must be lower than usual if we can hear it that well.'

'But why don't they synchronise them?'

'Not sure. It makes it harder to tell where they are, that's for sure. Or perhaps they just don't think it's worth the extra work. It'll be so high you won't be able to see it. First you'll know if it drops a bomb near you is the whistling sound.'

I felt my insides go cold, 'But that wouldn't give us time to evacuate people.'

'That's right. Too late by then.'

We were near a phone box and I went in to phone the ARP station. 'No,' they assured me, 'no raids due tonight. You've got first night nerves, Sweetheart, happens to sprogs all the time. Relax and get on with your round.'

Despite their patronising words, I felt the tension in my shoulders relax and my forehead unknot. A quiet night for my first duty was exactly what I'd hoped for.

I stepped outside the box to tell David the news when to my horror I heard the familiar whistling sound. It was terrifyingly close.

'Bloody hell!' David shouted, 'run for cover!'

It was too late to run and we threw ourselves to the ground, faces scraping on the road. I wrinkled my nose as I smelt tar and urine.

Then there was a crash so loud I thought my eardrums would burst, and a strong wave of air blew over us. But there was no explosion, and we looked around but saw no damage. There was a moment's silence, and we stood up feeling silly for having dived to the ground. Suddenly there was pandemonium as people rushed out of their houses, light spilling from a dozen doorways. 'What's happening?' 'Is this a raid?' 'Should we go to the shelters?'

Before we could answer, a young lad ran round the corner, 'Number 37's got it. Acacia Avenue. Bomb's taken off the whole bloody front of the house.'

'Less swearing, young man!' a woman's voice replied.

David and I took charge, and I was pleased my training made my reactions automatic. 'Okay everyone, it's unexploded so you need to evacuate. Get to your shelters straight away. Take your keys and hurry! It could go off any time.'

I went back to the phone box and told base what

happened, then joined David making sure everyone in the road was evacuated before heading to Acacia Avenue. What we saw stopped us as if we'd been punched in the stomach.

The front of a number 37 had completely disappeared. It looked like a child's doll house with the doors open. Each room, complete with its furniture, was as uncovered as a naked lady. Bricks lay amongst the tables and chairs, and pictures hung at wild angles or lay smashed on the floor. I quickly checked my list and found that the house was unoccupied. My relief that no-one had died in there made me stumble.

Brick dust filled the air, making us choke. Our eyes felt gritty and we rubbed them making them worse. We tiptoed towards the hole made by the bomb and looked down. My heart pounded so strongly it kept missing a beat. I held my breath as if exhaling would set it off and wondered if David was doing the same.

'Looks like a fifty pounder.' he said, 'let's get out of here and make sure the houses are empty.'

When we turned round we were surprised to find several other people peering into the hole too. 'Idiots! Get out of here!' David shouted, 'this could go off any moment. Go on! Now!'

Some of them hurried away. Others sauntered off as if to prove they couldn't be told what to do. Or to prove they were tough.

Sending up a prayer that the bomb wouldn't go off before we got to safety, we checked all the houses, then checked the ones in the street behind.

We knocked the last door in the road and it slowly opened. An old man in slippers and a dressing gown held onto the door frame for support. A gust of stale air followed him. 'I expect you want me to go to the shelter,' he said, his voice shaky and his shoulders slumped.

'Yes,' I said, 'there's an unexploded bomb in the next street. It could go off any time. Do you need some help?'

He shook his head, wringing his hands. 'No, I'm not coming. Vera was killed in last week's bombing raid. She got caught on the way back from the picture show. We were together forty years. I don't care if I die. Nothing to live for. You two go about your duty and leave me be.'

And with that, he closed the door. 'Mark him down as refusing to go to the shelter.' David said and we went on our way.

Other ARP volunteers appeared, along with the police and bomb experts. A police officer who looked important called us all together.

When we'd given our report he said, 'No point you all being here, you've evacuated the immediate area. Carry on with your duties. We could still have a heavy raid tonight. You can't be complacent.'

His voice carried such authority no-one thought to question him. What could we do anyway? We weren't bomb disposal experts. Other volunteers headed off in different directions towards the patches they covered. 'Let's go and have a cuppa,' I said, 'it's well overdue and my feet need a rest.'

Now the tension of the unexploded bomb had melted away, I realised I was dog tired and could barely get the energy to keep walking. David glanced at me, although he couldn't have seen much in such sooty darkness. 'You look exhausted. Come on, take my arm, we'll walk back to base together.'

His arm felt strong and comforting. Mostly though, I noticed the electricity between us. I'd heard of love at first sight but what I felt for David was an intense craving. I longed for him to take me in his arms, to be somewhere alone with him, to be close to him. I tried to remember if I'd felt like this with Edward, my fiancé. I was sad that although I remembered the few occasions when we were alone together, I couldn't bring to mind the emotions, the strong feelings that swirled through my body now. With David. Edward and I had never consummated our love. Lack of privacy and a fear of pregnancy always got in the way.

As always when I thought of David, I chided myself for my longings. I still didn't know if Edward, missing presumed dead, could still be alive. David never said anything to imply he felt the same about me, but if he did what would I do? If he did care for me and I gave in to my desire what would happen if Edward came back from war? I'd have let him down. Would he still love me and want to marry me? Although the truth was that I no longer knew if I still loved him, or just the memory of him. Or if I wanted to get married.

My thoughts were interrupted by David pulling my arm closer to his body so his upper arm pressed against my bosom. He stroked my hand gently. 'You okay, Sweetheart?' he asked.

'I'm fine, thank you.' I said. I was far from fine. My mind focussed entirely on his arm, the feel of it against my body, his hand stroking mine and his smell. He smelled of dust, some sort of cologne and his own smooth masculine skin that I longed to touch. I felt all hot and bothered and I could feel my body pulled towards him as if drawn by a magic spell.

David squeezed my hand, 'Lily, I wanted to say...'

He got no further when BOOM.

The bomb exploded.

We were knocked off our feet again, falling flat on our faces. I felt the skin on my cheek graze as it hit the road and my ears rang. Despite the noise and chaos, I felt David's arm over my shoulder, protecting me from the blast. The air around us swirled with debris drawn in by the force of the detonation and I was glad of my tin helmet protecting my head. I could hardly breathe, although it was hard to know if that was from the effects of the bomb or the effects of being so close to such an attractive man.

We lay there listening to the sounds of falling wreckage, and a gas main exploding some distance away. When the sounds died down, we turned to face each other, cheeks dragging on the ground. He kissed my forehead slowly and tenderly, and I lifted my face to be kissed properly. Although I'd only known him a short time, it was as if I'd waited for this moment my entire life.

But the kiss was not to be.

A scream punctured the moment and, like under water swimmers coming to the surface, we scrambled to our feet, hands clammy and white faced. Nearer to the bomb crater a woman was lying in the road, shrieking. Her breathing was sharp and shallow and her face was covered in dust and perspiration. She'd been dragged towards the crater by the force of the air filling the vacuum caused by the blast. Even though she was a good way from the crater, her clothes were rucked up exposing her legs which were burnt and bleeding. Her face contorted with agony and she looked at us without any real recognition that we were there to help her.

'Go and get an ambulance,' David said, 'I'll give her first aid.'

As I ran towards a phone box he was opening his first aid kit and taking out bandages and cream.

It took ten minutes for the ambulance to arrive. 'Was anyone with you?' I asked the injured woman, but she shook her head.

'I'll stay with her if you go and check for other casualties David. Is that okay?' He gave my cheek the lightest of kisses as he walked away and for a split second I brushed where his lips had touched before I gave the injured woman my full attention. There was little I could do but hold her hand and speak reassuringly.

My shift finished later than expected. No surprise with what had happened. Three people died and quite a few more were injured. We helped them into ambulances, happy to be relieved of the responsibility for caring for them and to see them in the hands of experts. Then we continued with our round. It had been an awful evening but not as bad the full-scale bombing other parts of London were experiencing.

'Did you see one of the people who died was the old man who refused to leave his house?' I said to David as we walked.

He nodded, 'It's sad, but perhaps he's with his Vera in heaven. Let's hope so.'

We reported back to ARP base for our area, filling in forms and talking over the experiences of the night. More experienced wardens were kind and congratulated us on the work we'd done.

As David and I were about to go our separate ways after signing off, I was surprised to see Alun, Bronwyn's brother, walk past. I introduced the two of them. Alun puffed himself up, greeted us as if seeing him the middle of the night were nothing unusual.

'You two courting then? he asked with a sly grin.

There was a moment's awkward silence then, 'No, we've

just been on duty together.' I said, then wondered why I bothered to reply at all, it was none of his business.

'Ah well,' he said, 'I must be on my way, things to do and all that.'

Tipping his hat he went on his way whistling cheerfully, a cocky spring in his step.

'I wonder where he's going this time of night.' David said, 'he can't be up to any good. And why hasn't he been called up? He's the right age.'

I turned to him, 'I've no idea, I'll ask him next time I see him. I've been meaning to ask, why haven't you been called up? You must be the right age too.'

He nodded, 'I tried, but they wouldn't accept me. I'm a scientist with skills they want, so I'm categorised Reserved Occupation.'

I knew better than to ask him what sort of scientist he was. If he was Reserved Occupation it was something top secret.

He took my hands in his, 'I've got to go away for a week on a work thing,' he said, 'but I hope we'll be on duty together again soon.'

He pulled me towards him and kissed me gently on the forehead. I wanted more, but had no idea how to let him know. I'd been bought up that nice girls never take the lead. Bronwyn would know, that's for sure.

I walked back slowly when my shift finished, barely able to drag one foot in front of the other. I thought back over the evening and the variety of emotions I'd experienced. More than anyone could expect in such a short space of time. It started with pleasure at being paired with David, then fear at the bomb dropping, relief when it didn't explode then absolute terror when it did. I'd seen more horror in one night than most people experienced in a lifetime.

My sleep was fitful. Scenes of dismembered limbs and people screaming filled my dreams. I woke again and again covered in sweat, so tired I desperately needed more sleep but was scared of what I'd see when I slept. I only got a couple of hours sleep before it was time to get up again to go to the depot. Bronwyn was still out for the count when I got ready to go, and she'd left a note saying not to wake her. But when I went into the living room, there was Alun spread across the settee, fully dressed, smelly feet and socks hanging over the arm. He was snoring gently. As usual, he'd left dirty dishes in the sink and stubbed out ciggies on a couple of them. They floated, damp and disintegrating, in the dirty water. Next to the settee was a rucksack I'd often seen him carry. The top was open and I peeked in. What I saw made me step back. There was a silver candlestick and a box. The box, probably for snuff, was elaborate with the initials BT on the top. And I could see part of a necklace that looked as if it was gold.

He was a looter. There could be no other explanation for it. It would explain why he was out in the middle of the night. The delayed action bomb David and I experienced was the only one to explode in our area. That meant Alun must have been in another part of London where they'd suffered more. There was a lot of talk about men like him. When others were trying to stay alive in shelters, they'd be out stealing from bombed houses and even from the bodies of the dead.

How dare he?

I stood and looked at him for a moment. He looked so innocent as he slept, but a wave of anger at what he'd done made my heart pound and my muscles quiver. I turned and grabbed the carving knife from the table, gripping it so hard my knuckles went white. Then I took a step towards him, my mind crazily blank, no idea what I was about to do. My arm was in the air, poised to plunge the knife into his chest, when he grunted and turned over. The noise and movement bought me to my senses and I slammed the knife down, picked up my things and left, resolving to speak to Bronwyn about him the next time I saw her. I couldn't stand the idea of him staying another night. And I didn't trust myself around him either.

On the bus to the Depot I couldn't believe what I'd just almost done. Committed murder. Had I lost my mind? Alun may have been getting away with looting but I'd never get away with killing him. I got out my bus ticket for the inspector and my hands shook so much he glanced at them, looked at me and said, 'You okay, Love?'

I couldn't speak. I opened my mouth but no words came out. I just nodded and he patted my shoulder and moved on down the bus.

I'd read somewhere that shock could have a strange effect on your mind and body. Had my madness over Alun come about because of the awful experience with the bomb exploding? I thought back over what I'd seen. Homes destroyed, that was bad enough. But the worst was the body parts. On films, dead people are always whole, even if they had a gunshot or stab wound. Their bodies were somehow neatly arranged. But an explosion randomly threw arms, legs and unidentifiable bits of body here and there. We had to help the other emergency services remove them, always taking care to try to identify people wherever possible. I soon learned to sort of switch off my mind as I undertook the gruesome work, but it left its mark. It was like holding a heavy weight for ages, muscles straining, then suddenly it's too much and the arm drops. Or the mind screams at the awfulness it just experienced.

I was relieved that Alun vanished for a couple of days and noticed his rucksack had gone too. Our rooms were too small for three people, especially when one of them wasn't too bothered about keeping himself or the place clean.

That weekend Bronwyn and I had chance to have a proper talk, the first for ages. It was a mild day and we wrapped ourselves up in coats and blankets and took our tea onto the rooftop outside our window, enjoying the peace that was only disturbed by the dull sound of traffic below. But the sight from there was depressing, with many ragged gaps in buildings. And it seemed that day by day London turned more grey.

'Bronwyn,' I said, my heart thumping, 'I need to talk to you about Alun.'

'Hey look,' she said pointing to a nearby window, 'that guy over there is getting undressed. You can see his underpants and everything. He's a bit of a hunk.'

I sighed, this was going to be difficult. 'Bronwyn, I need to speak to you about Alun.'

She turned to face me, 'The butter and eggs he gave us last week were a Godsend, weren't they? Help stretch the damn rations.'

I felt put on the spot. I'd eaten the butter and eggs too, so did I have a right to be feeling as I did about him? Did that make me as bad as him?

'Bronwyn, he's a looter.' I held my breath, expecting an explosion.

She merely nodded, 'Him and everyone else. Haven't most people picked up something left behind after a family have died or moved away after their place is bombed. I got a good novel last week, not a mark on it once I'd brushed off the dust.'

I rubbed my forehead and looked down, 'I'm not talking about little stuff, Bronwyn. Last time he was here I saw stolen stuff in his bag. A silver candelabra, a snuff box and what looked like a gold necklace. He must be going out during the bombing to get that stuff. He might even be getting some of it off dead bodies.'

She blinked fast, 'Taking things off dead bodies? He wouldn't do that.'

'Well, it's either that or he's breaking into houses. Look how much money he has to throw around and he doesn't have a job. I hate him being here. He's got to go. He was only supposed to be here for a few days anyway.'

She plonked her cup down and stood up. 'You can't tell me what my brother has to do. You've been glad enough to take stockings and food off him.'

'But Bronwyn...'

She glared at me, and gave an impatient snort, 'Enough! He may be a bit dodgy but he's my brother. He's not even here most of the time.'

'But the landlady said...'

She raised her eyes upwards, 'I know what she said. He could stay a few days, but she hasn't complained or said no to the stuff he gives her. Knows when she's on to a good thing and you should too.'

I took a deep breath. 'If it was just food and ciggies, I wouldn't be worried, but stolen stuff is another matter.'

'Oh, for goodness sake, Lily. It's all nicked isn't it? Stockings or snuff boxes or novels, it's all lifted. If you don't like it, you can always find yourself somewhere else to live.'

My chest tightened and I looked at her in disbelief. We'd been through so much together. Working in Paris, unmasking a German spy, the long escape to the coast. I thought we were like sisters.

'But Bron, if we have him here and the police find out what he's been up to, we could be charged as accessories. We could end up in gaol.'

She turned away from me and climbed back through the window, 'I'm going out. I hope you're more reasonable by the time I get back.'

Bronwyn hadn't been gone more than half an hour when Alun strolled in, ciggie hanging from the side of his mouth as usual. He plonked his rucksack down. I'd not long tidied and cleaned our rooms and the last thing I wanted was him making a mess of it all again.

'Make us a brew will ya, Doll?' he asked, 'Got some chocolate by yere in my bag. Nearly as sweet as you.'

'Make it yourself.'

He smirked, 'Tamping today, is it? Got the curse, have you?'

I leaned against the sink and folded my arms, 'I don't want your chocolate and I don't want you here with your stolen goods either. It's time you moved on.'

As if I hadn't spoken he stubbed out his ciggie, took off his shoes and socks and put his feet up on the settee. I could smell them from where I stood. He put his hands behind his head and closed his eyes, 'The tea can wait, I'll have forty winks first.'

I walked over and knocked his feet back onto the floor. He slowly opened one eye.

I put my hands on my hips, 'I said, it's time you moved on. I've had enough of your lazing about. Why haven't you been called up, anyway? You're not a restricted occupation, or any occupation at all as far as I can see.'

He sat up, scratched his privates, and smiled. Then he touched the side of his nose with his forefinger, 'Them in the know can get round the call-up. Know what I mean?'

I shook my head, 'How? Bribe someone? I wouldn't put it past you.'

'Nah, I just hand over a bit of dosh to some poor sod whose chest is so bad he'd never be called up. He pretends to be me. Easy as pie. Not being funny, but he's been a dozen other blokes so far.' He radiated superiority.

I could feel my heart beating fast at his total arrogance. I picked up his bag and threw it in his lap, 'Go on! Get out of here, you... you...'

He chucked the bag on the settee and lazily stood up. Then he took a step towards me, 'Come on, you don't mean it, Sweetheart. You love those stockings I bring, don't you? And you look good enough to turn on any red blooded man when you're wearing them.'

Without warning, he took a step forward and pinned me against the sink. He pushed against me, and grabbed me painfully between the legs, leaning forward to kiss me. His breath smelled of cigarettes and alcohol and made me want to heave.

But he'd reckoned without my ATS training.

I stamped hard on his bare foot and when he moved away a little, kneed him between his legs. Hard. He yelled 'Bitch!' and doubled over, groaning. I bent my arm and rapidly elbowed him in the face using the other hand to give extra force. Blood spurted out of his nose.

I opened the door, picked up his bag again and tossed it out into the corridor, along with his shoes. He was still clutching his nose and trying to breathe properly. I got behind him and pushed him out of the door, although he tried to resist. I'd learned how to deal with that too. I kneed the back of his knees just enough to make him unstable and after another hearty push he was out. I slammed the door behind him and shoved a chair under the handle to stop him getting back in.

Only then did I wonder how Bronwyn would react. My closest friend was about to become my enemy.

The air raid siren went off just as I began to drift into sleep. Cursing and only half awake I threw on some clothes and picked up the bag I learned to keep by the door. I'd lost track of how many nights in a row poor London had been bombed, and some other cities weren't having more luck. I'd been on ARP duty for the last two nights as well as working at the depot all day and hoped for a good night's sleep. Not that anyone in London ever got one any more.

I looked out for David as I scurried to the shelter and was disappointed to see he wasn't on duty. As always, the shelter was packed with people eating, chatting, drinking and trying to rest. I found myself a space and lay down, trying to get some sleep ready for a day at the depot. I'd spent ages trying to work out how to discover if anyone was stealing from there, but had no luck. I tried going amongst the men at different times, going round the site in different order and anything else I could think of but to no avail. I was always friendly and passed the time of day with them, but if the men knew anything they weren't saying. Maybe I should find out what pub they went to. People were usually more likely to give away secrets after a few beers. Trouble was, I could hardly go to a pub on my own. Bronwyn would probably never speak to me again after I threw Alun out so I couldn't ask her. I'd got more friendly with Edith who was still grieving over her missing husband. Maybe she'd like an evening out. I decided to ask her.

My gloomy thoughts were interrupted by a man nearby starting to play a mouth organ. Soon everyone was singing, *We'll meet again, There'll always be an England, Lily of Laguna* and others. It was just what we needed and took our minds off what was happening outside.

Sleep was a long time coming and I was just drifting off when the shelter suddenly shook and we heard the dull crump of a bomb dropping. It sounded louder than usual and dust drifted down from the ceiling. I flinched and looked up expecting to see cracks appearing but it all looked solid. Then another crump and another, and another, six in all, all nearby. After each crump there was a second or two's silence then several people groaned and a couple screamed. A baby nearby began to cry and its mother tried to comfort it.

The women nearest me gave a crooked smile, 'You been bombed out yet, love?'

I shook my head, 'Have you?'

'Yeah, two weeks ago. We've still been able to live in what's left of our house, but we've had no water, no electricity nor nothing. It's horrible. Lucky we've got good neighbours. They've been helping us out. Letting us have our weekly bath and things.'

I touched her hand, 'Do you have anyone you can stay with?'

She bit her lip trying to hold back a tear, 'Ain't got no-one, Dear. They're all gone. My last brother was killed in a raid a month ago. And me husband here, he's an only child. Any road, our jobs are here. If we moved out of London we'd have to start all over again and we're a bit old for that. You got family nearby?'

I thought of my mum and her awful boyfriend safe in Oxford. I decided to write to her again to try to patch things up. 'My mum lives in Sunbury, it's a suburb of Oxford. I'm in the ATS so I've been posted here. Have to go where you're sent.'

Another crump made us flinch, 'That sounds a bit close for comfort,' the woman said wrapping herself round with a blanket, 'Well, better try to get some sleep. Work tomorrow. Goodnight, dear.' She lay down and closed her eyes.

I slept badly and looked at my watch often. The air was stale and my head felt full of cotton wool. When I judged it was almost dawn I quietly picked up my stuff and headed towards the stairs. Climbing over people without disturbing them took ages. If the bombing was as bad as it sounded during the night, my ARP skills might be needed.

As I walked toward the entrance of the tube station the low sun sent weak rays through a cloud of dust. The air was full of smells: dust, fire and destruction. Barrage balloons drifted overhead like giant floating cartoon fish. I had to force my feet up the final few steps, scared of what I would find.

The street I'd left to enter the shelter was gone. Looking at the scene as if it were unreal, I felt my pulse raise until it seemed others around me would hear it. My palms became clammy and I took a big breath trying to calm myself. I licked my lips and found they were covered with a thin film of dust.

The houses around me looked as if they'd been flattened by an angry god. One or two still stood strangely untouched, while others were a heap of rubble or partly demolished. Sad belongings, once loved by their owners, lay amongst bricks, wood and pipes everywhere. Strangely the post box stood intact, standing higher than the chaos round it. Fires still burned here and there and firemen struggled to put out the biggest one further down the street. All around me people stood and gaped, unable to take in what was in front of their eyes. Some cried, others clutched their children to them glad to be alive. Several hurried off to see if their homes in adjacent streets were still standing.

Noise behind me told me more people were leaving the shelter. I stood aside as they emerged blinking and aghast.

A women standing near me cried out and staggered. I hurried to help her. 'All gone,' she kept repeating, 'everything gone, what shall we do?' Two young children clung to her skirts, their eyes wide and their bottom lips trembling.

I stood in front of her and took her hands in mine. 'Go to see the ARP warden over there,' I said looking her in the eye and hoping she could take in what I was saying, 'he'll tell you what to do. They have special stations set up for people in your position.'

Her eyes were distant as if reality was too hard to take in and I gently led her over to the warden. He took her by the arm, 'Sit down here, love, with your kids,' he said, gesturing to a curb, 'give me a minute and I'll help you get where you need to go.' He turned and looked at me, 'You can get off now, Sweetheart.'

As he spoke a man came rushing up to him, 'My son is in that house there,' he pointed to a partly demolished house, 'they hide in the cupboard under the stairs. Help me get them out. Pray we're not too late.'

While the warden went to get help I joined the man, whose name was Alfred, and we began the long task of clearing the debris. We had no tools and soon our hands were filthy and torn. It seemed that no matter how much bricks and debris we moved, the deadly pile grew no smaller. Dust flew up from the bricks making us choke, and every now and then we'd find a broken glass or other object the bomb had flattened. I found a bracelet and handed it to Alfred, hoping against hope that his daughter-in-law was alive so he could give it back to her.

Others came to help and I decided to see if my skills could be of use elsewhere. Two houses down I spotted an arm poking up from the rubble. I ran towards it. It was a woman's arm and she was wearing a wedding ring and a watch very like one my mother wore. My heart beat fast, surely she couldn't be alive under the rubble. The arm was all I could see.

I bent down and lifted her arm to feel for a pulse. For a second I couldn't take in what happened because the arm was too light. Then the horror of reality made me go cold and sweaty. The arm was not attached to her body. Where it had been pulled from her shoulder a bloody mess of muscles and tendons hung down dripping onto the ground. I gasped and dropped it. It fell with a dull thud on the broken bricks. Trying not to vomit I turned away and ran over to the ARP warden on duty to tell him what had happened, so stressed I could barely put a sentence together.

'She'll be a gonna,' he said, his face grubby and his expression grim, 'leave her and see if there's anyone else you can help. Concentrate on the living.'

I nodded, trying not to bring back the sandwich I'd eaten in the shelter, 'Where do we send the homeless?'

'Green Street school on Mortimer Road. A bus will come later to take them somewhere more suitable.' he said, then turned away as he heard a police car arrive.

I spent half an hour road directing people made homeless to the school. It was a difficult task. People were shell-shocked and didn't respond quickly to instructions. Many wanted to search for their belongings, but fires still burned here and there and many remaining bits of buildings were unsafe. Several times I had to urge people to leave the remains of their home and go to safety. When I gave one woman the address she wiped her face with a dusty hankie, 'You know it happens, but you don't believe it'll happen to you, do you?'

I was soon to understand what she meant.

It took a very long time until me and the other ARP people had done everything we could, and I was so tired I could hardly think straight. I walked towards home two streets away. The way there was still a jumble of bricks, wood, household belongings and paper and I had to look where I trod. The odd small fire from an incendiary bomb still burned bright. So I was concentrating on my safety when I turned the corner to my street. What I saw made me squeeze my eyes shut and put my hand to my forehead. The house where Bronwyn and I had rooms and the one next door were completely flattened. Dust drifted up from the rubble and a bed hung crazily at first floor level where a fragment of floor hung on like.a drunk trying to stay upright. My legs felt weak and my brain, already woolly from what had happened, refused to function. It was if my feet had been nailed to the road.

Then I felt a hand on my shoulder and a voice say, 'We're buggered, Lily, absolutely buggered.'

I turned and there was Bronwyn, lovely Bronwyn. I could have kissed her. I fell against her and threw my arms around her, sobbing, my legs feeling as if they were made of rubber. She clung just as hard to me. I tried to speak but my words choked with tears. I'd helped many people made homeless during my short time as an ARP warden, but now I truly understood what their despair felt like. After moving around from England to France and back again, neither Bronwyn nor I had accumulated a lot of stuff, but what we had was important to us. Our clothes, our few ornaments, our books and diaries. All gone. We didn't even have our uniforms to go to work in.

When our sobs quieted, we walked slowly towards the pile of rubble that had been our home. Our steps dragged, as if by refusing to reach what was left of the building, we could deny reality. Like so many people, we started to search amongst the debris hoping to find something belonging to us. A touchstone to our pasts. After a few minutes Bronwyn found a packet of Players cigarettes and the book she had picked up from another bombed house. A real irony. I found nothing at all belonging to me.

By the time all this had happened it was time to go to work, and we had to decide what to do. 'Let's find somewhere for breakfast first,' I suggested. Half an hour later we were sitting in a cafe eating bacon rolls and struggling to keep our eyes open. We weren't the only people looking worn out, it seemed most of the tables were full of people looking like they could sleep for a month.

'It's hard to know what to do first,' I said, resting my chin on my hand, 'find out where to get uniforms, go to work or find somewhere to sleep tonight. I was told to send people to Green Street school, I wonder if we should go there.'

Bronwyn wiped a smear of bacon fat from her chin, 'Why don't we go to work, then we'd have shown willing even though we'll be very late. They can decide about the uniform.' She looked at the sign showing the cafe opening hours. 'Let's meet back here at seven o'clock and decide where to sleep. It might be easier to just go to a shelter and find somewhere tomorrow.'

I grinned at her, 'No dates involving an overnight stay tonight then?'

She raised an eyebrow and side-swiped my arm, nearly spilling my tea.

'There's something I need to tell you, Bronwyn,' I couldn't look her in the eye.

She looked at me closely, 'Not being funny nor nothing, but you look real guilty whatever it is.'

'It's Alun. I threw him out. Forcibly. Probably gave him a bruise or two. He's been sponging on us too long and to top it all he tried to get handy with me. Very handy. I'd had enough.'

She sat back and folded her arms. I thought she was going to be angry with me, but instead she just laughed out loud. 'I wish I'd seen that. Couldn't have done it myself, mind, he's my brother after all, and if he told our mam I'd never hear the end of it. But I can't say I blame you.' she went quiet for a moment, 'He wasn't there when the house was bombed, was he?'

'I don't think so. You know him, he's probably shacked up with some girl or another.'

The day seemed never ending. I dragged myself to the depot and was immediately told to go and get myself a new uniform and other essentials. 'I don't expect to see you back here today.' the boss said, his voice full of sympathy.

I stopped in at the office and Edith was there alone. Mrs Rogan was somewhere else in the building and Marion was off sick.

'It's her monthly,' Enid said in a hushed voice, 'always affects her bad.'

I saw that Edith's eyes were red-rimmed, 'How are you, Edith?' I asked.

She promptly burst into tears.

'I haven't heard any more about Sidney,' she said, wiping her eyes with her lace-trimmed handkerchief. 'I miss him so much. I can't grieve for him when he might be still alive and I can't move on with my life. Not that I want to. I still love him. We wanted to start a family. Will I ever have nippers now? Sidney would be such a good dad.'

I sat down beside her and put my hand on hers, 'I'm so sorry,' I said, 'it's all so recent, no wonder you're all over the place.'

We sat in silence for a couple of minutes then she blew her nose and looked at me for the first time.

'Lily, whatever must you think of me. You with your Edward missing too.'

I started to say it was okay when she registered my clothes, 'Where's your uniform? What's happened? Don't tell me you got bombed?'

I told her all that had happened.

'I wish I could say come and stay with us, but the house is fit to bursting as it is. Will you be able to find somewhere?'

I nodded, 'Yes, don't worry about that, there are evacuation centres all over the place and tomorrow me and my friend Bronwyn will look for rooms again. We'll be okay.'

After chatting for a few more minutes and agreeing to go to the flicks together soon, we said our goodbyes and I headed for the nearest evacuation centre where I knew they'd have some clothes donated by kind Londoners. The school hall looked like a jumble sale was in progress and it smelled like one as well. There were tables laden with clothes and on the wall behind each table was a sign saying what they were 'Men's trousers,' 'girls' dresses,' and so on. But the sizes were all mixed up and it took a while sorting through them to find anything to fit.

Whole families were trying to get kitted out, with kids crying or rejecting the only things that fitted them. A lady standing next to me picked up a dress and inspected it closely, 'That'll do me nicely,' she said, folding it over her arm, 'it's better than any of the things I lost.'

When I'd found some clothes to keep me going, the kind volunteers gave me a cup of tea. I had my ration book because I always took it to the shelter with other important documents, but it had no coupons left. I thought with sadness of the jumper I'd bought not long ago, gone for ever.

'You coming back to sleep here tonight?' the head lady asked.

I shook my head, 'No, I've got to get myself a new ATS uniform then meet a friend. We'll find a shelter near there.' I went to shake her hand, but instead she gave me a big hug. It bought me to tears. When you're just holding on to your emotions by the skin of your teeth, kindness can be too much to stand. She took a step back and held my shoulders, 'You're a strong young woman,' she said, 'doing a difficult job. I wish we had more like you. Go now, I hope you find a uniform that fits!'

That bought a smile, there was no hope of a uniform that fitted in peace time, never mind in the middle of the Blitz. So I went to the address in central London I'd been given with little hope of something decent to wear, but good did come of it. Bronwyn was there, being handed her uniform, and I saw she already had a bag with some clothes beside her.

She waited while I got my uniform, then we asked where the nearest evacuation centre was.

The clerk was a middle-aged woman with a perm that was so tight her hair looked like it was made of corrugated card-board. She had a posh voice and spoke without looking up,

'Under John Lewis.' she said. When we didn't respond immediately she sighed heavily, 'I said, the evacuation centre is under John Lewis.' She finally looked up and waved us away with a flick of her wrist as if we were polluting her air.

I still expect her to laugh and say she was just kidding, but she simply carried on with what she was doing.

Bronwyn bent down so that her eyes were level with the woman's head and she couldn't be ignored. 'Are you serious? John Lewis? The department store in Oxford Street?'

The clerk looked up, 'That's right, but they won't be handing out free clothes you know.'

'Well, there's a turn-up for the books.' Bronwyn said as we turned away.

I looked at the clock on the wall. 'It's too early to go there now. Why don't we go to the flicks? It'll be dry and we can always sleep if it's boring.'

While we waited for the film to start I told Bronwyn about Edith's missing husband.

'So, both of you have missing men and no way of finding out more.' she said.

A few seconds later a man sitting in the row behind tapped me on the shoulder,

'Excuse me, Miss, but I couldn't help overhearing your conversation. The powers that be will tell you anything they know, but they can be slow and sometimes they don't know what the boys who were there knew.'

I turned round so I could see him. He looked like an old soldier, very upright posture and a kind but determined look, 'So what could we do?'

'What service is your man in?' he asked.

'He's a soldier.' A picture of him looking so smart in his uniform came to mind and I was strangely pleased. I was beginning to think I'd never recognise him if we ever saw each other again.

The man cleared his throat, 'If I was you, I'd go to his army base. Talk to the officials who have the records but ask around the men too. Someone might have seen something. It's worth a try.'

Just then the curtains opened and the film started.

'Thanks so much.' I said.

He patted my shoulder, 'Good luck. Hope you find him.'

We saw *Ten days in Paris* with Rex Harrison. It was an exciting spy thriller and kept us awake, although both of us nodded off through the B film. But it was warm and dry in the picture house and the advantage of seeing a matinee was there were rarely any air raid warnings to spoil the moment.

We blinked at the daylight when we came out, stretching our tired muscles and carrying our few belongings.

'Come on,' I said, 'I don't suppose there'll be food where we're sleeping. Let's go to Lyons and get some tea before we go there.'

We'd both been given a loan at work to see us over until payday. Just as well, because I had only a few coins in my pocket when I went down into that shelter. The thought made me pause. Was it really only last night that I left our rooms and headed to the underground? So much had happened that it felt like weeks ago.

We sat down at a small table with our tea and eggs on toast.

'Well,' said Bronwyn slumped over her food, 'this is a real turn up for the books and no mistake.'

I cut my toast, 'Soggy,' I said to no-one in particular, 'well, if this is hard for us just image what it must be like if you've got kids or an old person to look after. Not to mention we're still alive and not injured.'

'There's that, I suppose, we should count our blessings as my mam would say.'

We finished our tea and set off to Oxford Street. The afternoon was drawing in and we had to use our torches to find our way around. Some people were already heading for the air-raid shelters. Others still queued outside shops hoping there would be something they could spend their coupons on. Food became harder to find every day as more and more shops were flattened and roads became difficult to navigate.

A few yards from the shop we heard the sirens and the sharp whistle of the ARP warden telling us to take cover. Along with many other people we ran into John Lewis. The doors were open and staff shepherded us through the ground floor departments towards the basement. Once there, we found a space on the floor amongst the others who'd hurried to safety. The floor was covered in cardboard topped with a variety of materials: blankets and what must have been offcuts from fabric they sold.

We looked around, 'Bit different from the shop, that's all I can say,' whispered Bronwyn, 'all elegant upstairs. They haven't spent much money doing up this bit.'

I agreed but didn't like to seem ungrateful so I changed the subject.

Volunteers came round selling cold drinks and biscuits as well as some books and magazines. At first, it seemed like the only sound in the basement was the stirring of tea-spoons and the crunching of biscuits. But things soon changed and we were listening to the *crumps* of bombs outside, hoping none would hit the building directly and kill us all. Then, surprisingly, some Red Cross ladies came round offering wool and knitting needles. It broke the ice and soon the sound of needles clacking was hidden beneath chat and laughter.

'Reminds me of the baby cardigans I knitted for our Mavis,' 'Wonder if they'll let us take this away to finish?' 'Let's start a scarf to send to the boys.'

'Can you knit?' I asked Bronwyn, looking at the needles as if they'd bite me, 'Mum tried to teach me a couple of times but I never could get the hang of it.'

She took my wool and needles, 'Give it by yere, Cariad, I'll teach you. I've taught my sisters and they argued with me all the time, little buggers, so I'm sure I can teach you. It'll give us something to do.'

Two hours later when the All Clear sounded I'd managed three rows but somehow had five more stitches than I started with. Those people lucky enough to have a home to go to packed up their stuff and left us in the basement with the other homeless evacuees.

As they went it was easier to look around. For the first time I noticed some manakins in the corner. They were undressed and their limbs twisted at all angles with a couple of arms on the floor. The sight bought back memories of the lady's arm I'd picked up earlier. It was as if I was there all over again so vivid was the memory. The sight, sounds and smells of that awful moment overwhelmed me. I began to shake and could feel the tea and biscuits I'd just had rumbling in my stomach. I ran to the toilet and was violently sick. Even when there was nothing left in my stomach, I didn't dare move. My legs shook and my brow was filmed with sweat.

Bronwyn was waiting for me when I got out of the cubicle, 'What's up, Sweetheart?' she asked, wrinkling her nose at the smell of vomit in the air, 'not up the duff, are you?'

I walked over to the wash basin, rinsed out my mouth and washed my hands.

'There's no danger of that,' I said with a weak smile, 'It'd be the second virgin birth.'

Her jaw dropped. 'What, you mean you're still holding onto your cherry?'

Luckily there was no-one else in the Ladies or I'd have been far too embarrassed to talk about such personal things. 'Well, Edward's still missing...'

She raised her eyes to the ceiling, 'That's tough, can't argue with that, but who knows if he'll ever come back?'

She realised the implication of what she'd said, 'Sorry, Cariad, that was a bit insensitive of me. But didn't you tell me about a nice bloke you sometimes work with on ATS duties? David, was it? Sounded to me like you fancied him.'

I bit my lips, 'I do, but it wouldn't be right.'

She grinned, 'I've said it before and I'll say it again, lots of people are doing things that aren't right these days. Well, people used to think they weren't right, but things are looked at different these days. Look at me, I'm on my second married man...'

'Second! You didn't tell me that.'

'Well, not both at the same time. One moved back up north and then I met another nice bloke. He wines and dines me and I like him. No harm done. He'll go back to his wife and pick up where he left off soon enough.'

'What will you do then?'

She shrugged, 'I suppose I'll look for another one. I'm in no hurry to settle down.'

Just then two women came into the Ladies. We said hello to them and went back to our patch on the floor of the basement.

'I've never even been in John Lewis before,' Bronwyn said, 'far too dear for me.'

I grinned, 'Well, I've walked round once or twice but I couldn't afford anything either.'

We hauled our few belongings up the stairs from the basement of the shop and blinked in the daylight. The street looked much the same as normal. Well, normal for wartime with windows criss-crossed with tape and posters telling us that *careless talk costs lives*.

'We need to find new digs before we do anything else.' I said, 'any ideas where to look?'

Bronwyn pulled a map out of her bag. 'Tell you the truth, Cariad, I know a fair bit of London after riding around on a motorbike for weeks. We want to avoid the docks and anywhere else the Jerries will be aiming at. But we still need to be able to get to work.'

We spread the map on a wall and studied it. 'I think we should look here and here.' she said, stabbing the paper with her finger.

I didn't know either area, 'Where shall we try first?'

She thought for a minute, 'Tell you what, let's try by yere, there's a market on the way and we might pick up some second hand clothes and stuff.'

It was just a couple of stops on the underground then a twenty minute walk. The area wasn't as badly bombed as our last digs, but there was still plenty of damage to be seen. As we walked we saw five children sitting on a pile of rubble drinking tea supplied by WVS ladies, their faces and knees grubby. Two women scrambled through the same building looking for their belongings. One carried a big plant and another a mantlepiece clock. Despite what had happened to them, they shared a joke and their laughter lifted our spirits.

As we stood there three other women walked by, two

looked in their twenties and one was older, maybe their mother. They were well dressed but one was pushing a cart that looked like it was made of odds and ends of wood and a couple of pram wheels. In the cart was a suitcase and a bundle of things tied together with a sheet. The older woman carried a broom and a cardboard suitcase. A couple of boys under school age trailed along behind them looking tired and bored, their gas masks bouncing on their backs. They all walked with their eyes fixed ahead as if they'd collapse if they lost their concentration for a minute.

Bronwyn was right about the market. A patient horse stood attached to a cart while its owner called out 'Wet fish, Ladies, come and get your wet fish! Fish an' chips for the old man tonight!' Next to him a woman stood behind a hand cart selling vegetables. Her face was pinched and she was far too thin. I wondered how far she'd had to push the cart.

A few people had clothes and household goods on blankets spread on the road. We were sorting through them for anything half way decent that would fit when a movement caught my eye. I looked up and there was Alun, setting up a pitch for himself. He was wearing a tweed jacket and a trilby low over one eye. A cigarette hung from the corner of his mouth. He hadn't spotted us and opened the suitcase he was carrying. It was full of watches and jewellery.

'Come yere, Ladies!' he called in his Welsh accent, 'Treat yourself now. Or better still, treat your old man. Who knows what reward you'll get!' He swept his hand over his case like a magician. I nudged Bronwyn, 'Look, there's Alun. He's selling jewellery and stuff. Wonder where he got it from?'

Her head swivelled round from the jumper she'd been inspecting. She took in what he was doing and her shoulders slumped, 'I bet that's nicked stuff. Come on, we'd better let ourselves be known.'

He was showing a necklace to a woman and didn't see us walking towards him. But when he saw me, his jaw dropped and for a brief moment he looked terrified.

Bronwyn laughed, 'Gave you a good going over, did she?'

He drew his knees together in memory and his eyes hardened. 'What you two doing here, then? Why ain't you at work or at home?'

Bronwyn put her hands on her hips, 'Haven't been back there for a couple of days then?' she said, 'you're a bit out of date with the news. We're homeless. Bombed out. In fact, we're looking for someone to live now. Know anywhere?'

He paused so long we could almost hear his brain whirl, or more likely chug slowly. 'The couple who lived across the room from my girlfriend moved out this morning. If you're quick, you might be lucky.'

He'd just finished giving us the address when he looked over my shoulder and his body tensed. Moving quicker than I'd ever seen before, he closed the suitcase and ran into a side street with it tucked under his arm. We looked behind us and sure enough, there was a Bobby strolling through the market.

Bronwyn shook her head, 'What it is, that lad'll never change. He started nicking stuff when he was still at junior school and it looks like he's never stopped. Stupid sod.'

We went back to the stall where we'd been and she haggled with the women selling the jumper, did the deal, and shoved it in her bag. We were about to walk away when the lady said, 'Did you hear about Green Street School, over on Mortimer Street?'

It took me a minute to recognise the name then it came to me, that was where I'd been told to send evacuees the previous day. 'What about it?' I asked.

'Bombed flat,' she said, 'and full of evacuees, it was. 'undreds dead I 'eard.'

'What!' I said, my voice hoarse, 'They were still there? Buses were supposed to move them somewhere safer.'

'I can only tell you what I 'eard, love. Buses never turned up and they all bought it, every single one of 'em. God 'elp them.'

I covered my face with my hands and sobbed, clutching Bronwyn's arm. 'What is it, Cariad?' she asked, supporting my weight.

'I... I... I sent loads of people to that school yesterday, just before I met you. The ARP warden told me to send them there.'

She gasped, 'Oh my God, Lily, that's awful. Those poor people. But it's not your fault. You just followed orders. What else could you have done? You couldn't know what would happen.'

'But why didn't the buses come?' I sobbed, remembering the woman I'd spoken to and and her children.

She pulled my arm closer to her and walked forward, taking tiny steps. 'We'll never know, Cariad. But you helped them as best you knew. It was someone else who didn't do their job.'

I wiped my eyes but my heart felt heavy. So many deaths, children as well as adults. Would it never end?

'Come on now,' Bronwyn said, 'Let's go and look at those rooms or now after we'll spend ages hunting. Let's hope they're not already gone.'

Finding somewhere to live in London was harder and harder as more and more houses were bombed, so we didn't have much hope. But we were lucky, the rooms were still free and they were much the same as the ones we'd left. We paid our first week's rent and then looked around working out what we'd need just to get by.

'We should get back to that market double quick,' I said,

'let's hope someone is selling some sheets and towels. Tell you the truth though, I'm not too keen on living so close to Alun again. He's a user.'

Bronwyn shrugged, 'You're right. He'll probably fall out with the girlfriend and try to scrounge off us again. We'll be stronger this time if it happens.'

'So, what act can you do?' Jim asked, 'Sing? Dance? Read poetry? Play the piano?'

Our regional ARP unit was putting on a Variety Show. Fed up with criticism from members of the public who thought we did nothing but moan about lights showing in their homes during the blackout, we decided to do something to give us a better image. It would cheer us and everyone else up too.

The Ritz cinema agreed to let us have an hour and a half after the Saturday morning pictures for kids and before the film matinee started. Jim, the head ARP warden for our area, called a meeting to decide who was doing what. It was the first time I'd met many of the other wardens because our shifts hadn't coincided. After an hour of discussion, sometimes verging on arguments, we agreed a program. It included two comedy sketches, a magician, two singers singing four songs between them, a dance routine and a song by a school choir. Jim would compare and tell some jokes. With a flourish he reached down to a bag next to his chair and took out a top hat and bright red waistcoat. He put them on and twirled round waiting for applause. It was a side of him I'd never seen before.

'You'll look like a circus master!' someone quipped.

Jim grinned, his missing front tooth more on display than

usual. He tapped the side of his nose. 'Well, maybe I was before I retired. That's for me to know and you to guess. Now, what talents have you lot got?'

Half an hour later David and I were assigned a comedy sketch Jim had written. 'I used to write for Bob Hope I'll have you know.' he said as he handed us the script.

No-one believed a word of it.

But when David and I settled ourselves at the *British Queen* with our drinks: half a shandy for me and a pint of bitter from him, we wondered if he might be telling the truth. The script he'd given us was quite funny. Or would be if we could act it well enough.

The pub was busy and we struggled to find seats where we could hear each other. A darts match was going on in one corner amidst great hilarity and not a little cursing. A couple were having an argument and the woman suddenly threw the dregs of her drink in the man's face and stormed out. Several old men watched impassively as they nursed their half-pints, clay pipes clenched in their gums. Three older women, still wearing their outdoor coats and sporting hair nets, sat gossiping as they sipped their cider.

We settled in our seats and read through Jim's script deciding who would play which part. I noticed as we spoke that our our bodies moved in unison, when I moved a certain way, he did too, and vice versa. Then as we laughed about something our knees suddenly touched. It was as though the air grew warmer. Without thinking I undid the top button of my blouse, then felt embarrassed and hoped he hadn't noticed. As he moved to hold his glass I noticed as if seeing them for the first time, the hairs on his lower arm, soft yet manly. My knee felt so charged, I thought it would never feel normal again. I wanted to look at him to see if he'd noticed but didn't dare. His hand moved towards mine, then back to where it had been. An awkward silence descended on us as if a thick fog blocked out all sound.

After a pause that probably lasted a couple of seconds, but seemed like hours, we took sips of our drink at the same time. David cleared his throat, 'Heard anything from your fiancé yet?' he asked.

The question bought me back to my senses and numbed the hormones that were threatening to overpower my good intentions. 'No, he's still missing, but I keep hoping he'll be found. It does happen.'

He nodded, 'It must be very difficult for you, holding out hope all this time.'

'It would be harder not to have hope though.'

The atmosphere between us changed again and I found I could hear the noises around me in the pub again. The clatter of glasses, the darts hitting the dartboard, the chatter, the door opening and all the other everyday sounds that had faded away.

'Come on,' David said, his voice brisk, 'let's make a start. We've got a lot to learn and not much time to rehearse what with work and different shifts.'

I scraped my hand through my hair, 'We may need to meet up at other times.'

He smiled and his eyes told me how much he liked that suggestion, 'Yes, we might.'

~

The next evening I was on ARP duty and thrilled to find David was on duty with me. The air raid sirens sounded early; some people weren't even home from work. David and I helped people get to their shelters; supporting the lame, encouraging the slow and trying to comfort the terrified. All the time, the sky was lit by anti-aircraft bullets sending streaks of light through the darkness to bring down planes so high overhead we couldn't see them at all.

When the streets emptied, we did our rounds, knocking on doors to ensure no-one was accidentally left behind. We could see several other parts of London were ablaze, the now familiar red lighting the sky telling its story of death and destruction. Relieved our patch had escaped so far, David and I went back to the ARP post to report in.

We'd no sooner finished our report and made ourselves a cup of tea when a Jerry plane dropped a load of incendiary bombs nearby. We all rushed outside, taking buckets of sand and stirrup pumps with us. All around us the incendiaries flared with flames so bright they lit up the streets. Sometimes the fires were on the road and were easily put out, others hit houses and set roofs alight.

David and I saw one roof blazing and knocked on the door in case the family were hiding under the stairs as people often did. Still wearing her wrap-around apron, the lady of the house came to the door. 'What is it?' she asked as if we were Bettaware salesmen disturbing her peaceful evening to sell her some plastic boxes or a new broom.

'Your house is on fire.' we said, pushing her aside.

'No, it's not!' she shouted after us, 'you come back here, you bleeding tin-pot dictators!' As we went past the living room door we saw, to our amazement, an elderly man sitting in an armchair. His eyes were open but there was no sign of a reaction to the blaring siren or us moving around. Maybe he was deaf. Or lost his mind. 'Get him under the stairs,' David shouted to the stroppy woman, but got no reaction from either of them.

She followed us upstairs, muttering away that we were

invading her house, but stopped when she saw a corner of the bedroom ceiling was glowing red.

'Fetch a broom.' I shouted to her as we moved the bed out of the way.

'Save the carpet, save the carpet!' she shouted as she hurried downstairs. A minute later she was back. She handed me the broom and kept chanting, 'Save the carpet! Save the carpet!'

I handed her the tin bucket, 'Fill that with water. Now!' she scuttled off as if her life depended on it. In no time at all she was back struggling under the weight of the water.

'Go back down and get under the stairs. Leave this to us!'

'Remember my carpet!' she said, hurrying out of the door.

'Bugger the carpet.' David said when she'd gone back downstairs. He poked the ceiling with the broom and jumped back. That section collapsed, incendiary bomb and all, and we set about putting it out. He used the water pump and I directed the hose at the fire, but it was beginning to spread. We grinned and grabbed the carpet, using it to help extinguish the flames.

'Needs must.' I said, suppressing a giggle.

Back downstairs we found the elderly man still sitting in the chair as if nothing was happening. 'I wonder if he's dead.' I said and went to check, but he was breathing easily and seemed to be asleep.

I knocked on the door of the cupboard under the stairs. It opened an inch. 'Fire's out.' I said, 'but you'll need to get that roof protected tomorrow.'

She stuck her head out, 'Is my carpet okay?'

Without answering we left and headed towards the street to put out more blazes. Outside we shared a conspiratorial grin. David linked arms with mine and, like children, we skipped a few yards before we saw another fire needing our attention.

Stepping apart we ran towards it. It was a small fire, easily put out using the sandbags that were placed at regular intervals down the street. As we stood to stretch our backs a movement caught my eye. I turned and there, moving in a house that was badly damaged by fire, was Alun.

I nudged David, 'I know that bloke, he's my friend's brother and he's looting.'

Alun hadn't seen us.

'Want to nab him?' David asked.

'Let's just give him a fright.'

We strode over, shining our hooded torches in his direction. Now the fires in the street had been damped down, they showed in the gloom.

'Oy, you!' I shouted, 'you're under arrest for looting!'

Alun jumped as if someone shot a starting pistol next to his ear. He grabbed his bag and ran fast enough to be in the Olympics. I doubt he even knew it was my voice. It set me thinking what it must be like to be him. Cocky on the outside, always with a quick put-down or joke. But on the inside? I couldn't imagine having watch my back all the time for fear that the law would grab me. Or the army would realise I didn't have a bad chest. Or some of his crooked friends decide to get back at me for something he did wrong. He thought he had an easy life, but it seemed anything but to me.

'You okay with that?' David asked and I grinned. 'It won't stop him, but maybe he'll be a bit more careful in future.'

'Dangerous game to play, looting while buildings are unsafe. He could get caught in an exploding gas pipe or a building could fall on him.'

'He thinks he's immortal. For Bronwyn's sake I hope he keeps safe. Doesn't help the people he steals from though.'

The station was packed. Families moving out of London carried as many belongings as they could while they tried to keep hold on their wriggly kids; soldiers with kitbags over their shoulders smoked and chatted to each other and people looked anxiously at the timetable hoping to meet loved ones off the train. They'd probably have a long wait. Trains were so disorganised there was never any way of knowing when one could come or even if it would ever arrive.

I'd got my kitbag with me and was on my way to Oxford to visit Mum. We'd barely been in touch since I told her about her boyfriend's behaviour. If she was still with him, it was going to be a quick visit. But I could go to see my friends and maybe go to the Picturehouse to see my old boss.

The toot-toot of the train warned me it was pulling into the station and we all pushed forward, hoping for a seat. But I was out of luck, the train was already full and even with some people getting off there wasn't a seat to be had. I found a gap in the corridor, put down my kitbag and sat on it.

Soon everyone in the corridor was chatting. 'Where are you going?' another ATS girl next to me asked. She was pretty with dark curly hair many film stars would have been proud of.

'Oxford, to see my Mum.' I said.

She looked at me, 'You look a bit glum about it. Don't you get on?'

'Normally we do...'

'But...?'

I bit my lip, wondering whether to tell her about Mum's boyfriend. She had a warm, friendly personality and I thought I'd never see her again so decided to come clean.

'It's her boyfriend. He tried to get fresh with me.'

She frowned, 'Bloody Nora, that's a bit rich. Did you tell your Mum? I bet she'd throw him out.'

'I did,' I said, my chest aching with the memory of our conversation, 'she didn't believe me. We had a row and I haven't seen her since.'

She put her arm round my shoulder, 'That's tough, Love. Think he'll still be around?'

The comfort of her arm helped eased my anguish, 'I don't know. If she's written to me I probably wouldn't have had the letter what with being bombed out and everything.'

Before she could answer there was a terrible sound of metal on metal and we were thrown sideways with a shuddering jolt. For a minute I couldn't understand what was happening. Then I realised the train had catapulted off the track. Our carriage landed to the right with dreadful creaks and groans. Strange angles made it hard to take in what was what; what was floor and what was ceiling. Everything was changed.

All around us people were thrown on top of each other and bags flew here and there as if they had a life of their own. A few people screamed and a baby nearby cried. The ATS girl landed on top of me, taking all the air out of my lungs, and a soldier the other side of her landed on her legs. People inside the carriages were thrown towards the windows and doors, their faces squashed and their bodies crushed by others falling on them. Several people looked unconscious and some had bloody faces, the red smearing the glass.

The girl I'd been talking to and I struggled to free ourselves from each other, not a word between us: shock stealing our tongues. For what seemed like an age, I just lay there, on my back, legs having no floor to stand on. Then

Moira, the girl I'd been chatting too, groaned and I came out of my trance.

'Come on, girl,' I thought, 'use your ARP training.'

As I turned, my movements made the metal complain worryingly. I knelt, trying not to put weight on the window that was now the floor. It was cracked in several places where the impact of the train falling had punched stones through it. I noticed the next window was as smashed and straggly clumps of dirty grass poked through.

People were suddenly all talking at once and trying to get themselves the right way up. In the carriage next to where I was someone managed to open the door and two people fell on top of those in the corridor. Several people yelped in pain or swore loudly.

I stood up and, taking tiny steps on the uneven surface, went to where Moira had been thrown. 'Are you all right? What's happened?' I asked.

'It's my ankle,' she said, clutching it, her face tense with pain. She nodded her head towards the soldier who had moved himself off her, 'he fell on it.' He'd banged his head and was looking in a daze. His scalp was bleeding and blood dripped down his face making him look like something from a horror film. I left Moira for a minute and looked at his wound, relieved to find it was smaller than I'd though it might be.

'Got a hankie?' I asked the soldier. I had to asked three times before he took in what I said then he reached into a pocket and found a none-too-clean one. It would have to do. I folded it up so the cleanest bit could be used and pressed it on the wound. Then I put his hand over it, 'Keep your hand there!' I ordered.

Keeping an eye on him I turned to Moira. I felt her ankle and got her to move her foot in circles and then wriggle her toes. 'I don't think it's broken.' I said, hoping I knew what I was talking about, 'Just a nasty bang. You'll have a good bruise there tomorrow.'

I turned round and stood up as best I could. 'Any doctors or nurses here?' I shouted.

There was a knocking on the window of the next carriage. 'I'm a nurse.' a woman shouted, but she was stuck fast by the bodies of the people who had been sitting next to her. They'd been thrown against the windows and doors like everyone else in carriages. Two were unconscious, a couple had bloody heads and some clutched their arms or heads.

It was impossible to do much. They couldn't get upright, squashed as they were, and their floor was now a wall. The window and door was the floor and ominous creaking sounds showed that the weight of four people was more than the glass was designed for.

The nurse tried, painfully slowly, to get free of the people on top of her. A plump older woman in a green knitted hat had been thrown onto the door and blocked her way. She was unconscious and blood trickled from a cut on her forehead and out of her nose. The nurse tried to push her aside, but there was nowhere for her to go; other bodies took every bit of space.

Then the worst happened. The glass cracked, cracked some more, then gave way and all five people who'd been sitting in that side of the carriage slid towards me and Moira. I yanked Moira out of the way and we landed on top of the soldier who'd fallen on her. We watched helplessly as the five people fell into the corridor with a heavy thud and pitiful groans and cries.

The nurse was under the others, but miraculously had slid sideways so she was able to extract herself from the heap of limbs and unconscious people. I pulled her upright and held her until she got her balance.

We looked around. It was like a battle scene. People lay in heaps or struggled to get upright. Some were only winded, but others were in a much worse state. Bags, glass and assorted belongings were strewn here and there.

'Okay,' I shouted, 'if you can hear me and you're injured or next to someone unconscious, put your hand up.'

I had to repeat the message a couple of times until I was sure everyone had heard me over the noise of the train moving as people stood or sat up.

'Let's see who's in the worst state.' the nurse said. She looked at me, 'Let's hope help will be here soon,' she said, 'but we'll do what we can.'

We'd only taken a couple of steps when there was a terrible screeching sounds and the train slid further down the slope we were on before settling again. Several people screamed and the nurse and I fell painfully to our knees.

We struggled to get to those who needed help because of the uneven 'floor' and the heap of people blocking our path. The nurse took the lead and I helped her when possible, but there wasn't a lot we could do without any bandages. Mostly, we tried to reassure people.

It seemed like hours later when we heard the sound of emergency vehicles. 'Thank God,' the nurse said, some of the tension leaving her face, 'help is on the way.'

Before long someone bashed on the side of the train, 'We'll be back soon!' a man's voice shouted, 'keep calm!'

But it was another twenty minutes before they got to us.

Meanwhile the nurse and I continued to do what we could to help people. A little boy, blond and beautiful, was dead, crushed by the weight of bodies falling on him. His mother rocked him in her arms, sobbing as her heart broke. A middle aged woman held them both, rubbing the mother's back and speaking quietly. I wondered what she could be saying. An elderly man died too. He'd been on top of other people and looked uninjured, 'Probably a heart attack.' the nurse said, quietly closing his eyes and putting a cloth over his face.

As the firemen started to help us I turned to the nurse, 'If two died in this bit of the carriage, I wonder how many altogether on the train.'

Her chin trembled, 'We did what we could, we did what we could.' she said, her voice shaking, tears rolling down her cheeks. She clutched my hand and we hugged as best we could.

Eventually all the people who could walk were pulled out, although the action of being rescued caused more injuries as they were forced through small spaces. Clothes were ripped and arms and legs cut. But, like us, they were glad to be alive. Not everyone was so lucky.

Moira and I sat on the side of the rail track under dark clouds and it started to drizzle, icy specks finding a way to make our day even worse. As we sat it gradually soaked and chilled us completely. The rescue services handed out some ground sheets but there weren't enough to go round and we used them to protect the most injured until an ambulance could take them to hospital.

An hour later, having given my name and address, I made my way to the road, trying to find a way to get to Oxford. We were about a mile from a village but no buses were due until the next day. I hoped someone would offer me a lift, but the ambulances and police were all too busy helping the injured. I'd got a lot of bruises, but other people were in a much worse state. There was nothing for it but to walk. My legs were so weak every step felt like a mile and my kitbag got heavier with rain and exhaustion.

It must have only been about a mile to the village. I went to first pub I saw hoping to get a room. The sight of the cheerful bar felt like another world. A fire blazed gold and yellow against one wall, men played darts in the other bar and old men, still wearing their caps, played dominoes next to the fire. The bar smelled of beer, cigarettes and damp clothes. Even in my cold, wet state my shoulders relaxed a bit and I dropped my kitbag where I stood.

I went to the fire and warmed my hands while several people looked on. 'You been in that train crash?' one of the domino players asked. I could only nod.

'Rum do, that,' he said, 'someone'll have their guts for garters over that, you mark my words.'

A woman came over and handed me her glass of stout. 'Get that down you, girl. It'll help warm you up.' She took a handkerchief out of her massive handbag and gently wiped dirt from my face. I stood there like a child, letting her look after me, tears rolling down my cheeks. When she's finished I touched her arm, 'Thank you so much.' I said, and briefly squeezed her hand.

'Come and sit with us if you want to.' she said. I looked across at her table. Three other ladies all in their sixties or seventies sat there in their hats, hands wrapped round their glasses. They all smiled and made sympathetic noises.

'I need to sort out a room, but thanks very much.' I replied.

I moved over the bar where the landlord was pulling a pint.

He looked up and his jaw dropped, 'Whatever's happened to you, my dear?' He said, 'you look like you've really been in the wars.'

'I was in the train crash.' Just saying it made me want to cry again. 'Have you got a room please?'

His face dropped, 'I haven't, love, others got here before you.' He gave me a free half of shandy, 'You can sleep in the bar if you like through. There's benches against the wall. I'll see if I can find you a blanket.'

His wife came through from a back room and saw my bedraggled state, 'Oh my goodness,' she said, 'here, give me your wet uniform. I'll lend you an old dress and hope your things dry by the morning.'

She led me through to their rooms above the bar. The living room was warm and cozy with a fire burning in a small grate. Toby jugs stood on every available space. There must have been twenty of them. She saw me looking, 'They're me old man's,' she said, pulling a face, 'I hate the things myself. Dust collectors. But come with me and I'll find you something to wear. I'm Mrs Wilkes by the way, but I don't like to be formal, so call me Susan.'

She found me a warm dress, a thick cardigan and a blanket. Then she took one of the cushions off her settee and we headed back to the bar.

The group of ladies bought me another drink and a pork pie and I was asleep before the bar had even emptied.

Next morning the sound of beer kegs being moved woke me and I sat up, bleary eyed. The landlord saw me, 'You're a real sleepyhead,' he called, 'get yourself upstairs. The missus will give you some tea and toast if you ask nicely.'

Using the blanket as a dressing gown I went upstairs and noticed that a couple of bedroom doors were empty where others had made an early start.

Susan was busy tidying the living room, 'You look a lot better than yesterday,' she said, straightening the cushions on the settee. 'Want some breakfast?'

As I sat at her small kitchen table, I noticed a tin of corned beef on a cabinet and my hand holding toast stopped half way to my mouth. I recognised that tin. It came from Army stores although I couldn't tell if it was from the depot I worked at or another one.

Susan saw me looking and smiled, 'That was a bit of luck, that tin. One of the blokes who took a room last night gave it to me. He'd been in the train crash too. Must have got away a lot quicker than you though. Gave me that tin of beef as a tip. We'll enjoy some Corned Beef Hash for our tea tonight.'

I took a bite of my toast although I couldn't taste it at all. I remembered my mission to find out who might be stealing from the depot.

'That's interesting. It's an unusual brand. Not sure I've ever seen that one before. I wonder where he got it from.'

Susan shrugged, 'Dunno, he didn't say and these days you don't look a gift horse in the mouth, do you.'

'I wonder if I met him on the train. Me and a nurse helped a lot of people. What did he look like?'

She looked up trying to remember. 'Didn't take a lot of notice to be honest. I was busy when he had a bite of breakfast. I remember he was tall and a bit foreign looking. A bit dark like he was Italian or something. Does that ring a bell?'

'Did he have an accent?'

She shook her head, 'Not that I noticed, but he didn't have much to stay for himself, know what I mean?'

I shook my head but the truth was we had two or three men at the depot who could fit that vague description. I'd need to do a bit more detective work when I got back to work.

Next day it took three buses and four hours but eventually I made it to Oxford, dreading the reception I would find.

I walked towards Mum's house and realised I no longer thought of it as my home, even though it was the only permanent place I could give that name. My footsteps dragged and not just because of all I'd been through in the last twenty four hours. My breathing became rapid and shallow as I tried to think of the various ways meeting her could go. Was Alex, the dreadful boyfriend, still there? If so, it must mean she still didn't believe me. Or worse, she didn't care. But I couldn't believe that of her, she'd always been a loving mother. If he was gone, it could be for some other reason, so she might still think I lied. My best hope was that she'd found out what he was really like and thrown him out.

I knocked on the door, tentatively as first, then more firmly as no-one responded. She was out. I didn't know whether to be pleased or not, but the tension in my shoulders relaxed a little. I looked around the garden. She'd been busy making what was a mess with bricks and rubble left behind by the builders into something that was restful to the eye, even in cold weather.

I knew where she kept the spare key; under a plant pot at the side of the house. I fetched it and let myself in. The smell of the house, furniture polish and mum's cooking, hit me in a way nothing else could and caught my throat. I walked through to the kitchen and dumped my kitbag down, rubbing my sore shoulders. I put the kettle on, then went upstairs to Mum's bedroom. If anything would show if the ratbag was still there, it would be his clothes in the wardrobe.

I sent up a little prayer as I opened it, then let out a sigh of relief. There were no men's clothes there. Just to be sure, I checked the drawers and then my old room. Nothing. Mum still might not believe me but at least I wouldn't have to put up with that awful apology for a man and his devious ways.

I was on my second cup of tea when I heard the key in the lock. Holding my breath, I walked towards the front door. Mum gasped and stood still for a second when she saw me, her eyes widening. I held out my arms, wondering if she'd knock them aside, but she ran forward and wrapped me in a comforting embrace. She smelled of her favourite Lavender toilet water and soap and the smell took me back to childhood and happier days.

'Oh Lily,' she kept saying, her voice breaking, 'I'm so glad you're home.'

She looked just the same, her warm brown eyes and wavy hair. She was wearing a dress I hadn't seen before. She saw me looking, 'Got it in a jumble sale last week. Only took a little while to make it fit.'

I made her some tea and we sat while she asked what had happened in my life since we last met. She was horrified to hear about the bombing and the train crash.

'Didn't you get my letters?' I asked.

She frowned, 'No. I thought you didn't want to write or having anything to do with me. Alex...'

I folded my arms, 'I see that Alex has moved out. When did that happen?'

She leaned forward and put her hand on my arm, 'About two weeks ago. I...'

'Finally believed me? I bet he hid the letters, the bastard.'

She nodded, 'I've been such a fool. After your dad, I was so glad to find someone who wanted me, I suppose I ignored things I should have noticed and done something about it.'

I put the kettle on again, 'What made you finally get rid of him then?'

She cleared her throat and rubbed the back of her neck, 'I'd been hearing little things about him on and off, but nothing I could have a go at him about. Then...'

I raised an eyebrow, 'Then, what?'

'I came home early from work one day and caught him in bed with someone else. She was a lot younger than me too. Probably not as old as you even.'

'Bloody hell, Mum, what did you do?'

She gave a wicked grin, 'They didn't see me at first. I crept downstairs and got a bowl of cold water, Chucked it over the pair of them. Naked as the day they were born, they were, everything on show, his bum in the air. I'd never noticed before how hairy it was! The water cooled them down a bit, I can tell you. You've never seen two people move so fast. Took me days to dry out the bed but it was worth it.'

It took me a minute to stop laughing. I wished I'd seen it. Or maybe not. 'Did Alex go willingly?'

She laughed, 'Nuh, only tried to talk me round, didn't he. Like I'd ever forgive him. My own bed too! Even when I was throwing his clothes out of the window into the front garden he was trying to smooth talk me. Fat chance! Whatever did I see in him?'

'I wondered that. Next time you find a man, you've got to let me see him before you get in too deep.'

'Hang on a minute. I'm still your mum, you know. Anyway, any news of Edward?'

'Not a word, but I'm going to see his mum and dad tomorrow to see if they've heard anything.'

She frowned, 'But surely they'd have told you?' The look on her face showed what she thought of them.

That reminded me, 'Oh, I haven't told you. We got bombed out. Our place was totally flattened. So if they wrote there, I won't have got it. I'll give you our new address. Me and Bronwyn are still sharing.'

I went to bed that night in my old room relieved that me and Mum were back to normal. After being close all my life,

I hated having hard feelings between us. We'd put up with a lot of difficult times with my dad and who knew what the future held?

The next day I visited old friends and even saw my old boss at the Dream Palace, the picture house where I worked before I joined up. My last visit was to Edward's parents. Our road used to be divided in two by an eight-foot wall with barbed wire on top. While we lived in a Corporation house, on the other side were the posh houses, privately owned, and Edward's family lived in one of them. The people that end didn't want us walking through their end of the road and the wall caused a lot of anger with us Corporation house people. Eventually, after a lot of campaigning, the wall was taken down much to Edward's mum's disgust. A snob through and through, she looked down on me, but his dad was okay although he never said much or stood up to her as far as I could see.

I knocked on the door remembering times I'd done this in the past. I was disappointed when Mrs Halpen opened it. 'Oh, it's you.' she said, like I was something she'd scrape off her shoe. She didn't invite me in.

'I wondered if there is any news of Edward.' I said, working hard to keep my voice confident.

She held onto the door as though I might try to push my way through. 'No. None.'

I took a bit of paper out of my bag. 'I've moved. Here's my new address or you can write to me via the ATS head-quarters.'

She snatched the paper out of my hand and started to close the door. But before she did it I said, 'I hope we can be friends for Edward's sake, as well as yours.'

There was no reply. I was talking to the door.

'And one, two, three, four...'

It was the third rehearsal for the ATS show and Jim was in his element, bossing us all about and encouraging us to get our bit of the show just right.

It was the first time we'd rehearsed in the picture house. Being there with no film on the screen felt strange, even though I'd worked in one before. But then, the show had always just started or finished and I'd had a job to do. Our voices echoed round the auditorium but I knew when the place was full it would sound different.

David tried out some jokes on me. He stood straight and saluted:

'Hitler and Goring stood on top of the Berlin radio tower."

"I want to do something to put a smile on the faces of the people of Berlin." Hitler said.

'Then why don't you jump?" Goring replied.

'*A Nazi official is driving in the countryside when he runs over a pig. He can't see the owner so he goes to a nearby beer house to enquire. He opens the door, makes a Nazi salute and shouts, "Heil Hitler, as swchwin ist tot.' There is a moment's silence then a loud cheer and the bar owner says drinks are on the house.*

After five more jokes I was clutching my sides from laughing so much. I'd learned a couple to tell, but most of our time was a short sketch about living with bombing every night. After all, it had its less serious side too. People were much more open minded about all sorts of things they disapproved of before the war started.

We watched as Jim called out to the dancers. They high-kicked as they linked arms like Busby Berkeley girls. 'Come on girls, SMILE!' Jim shouted. Two of the girls poked their tongues out at him, but he pretended not to notice. They looked pretty good to me.

'Only one more rehearsal after this,' David said, 'you feeling ready?'

'Well, I know the words, but whether I can say them in the right order in front of an audience is another matter.'

He put his hand on mine, 'We'll keep practising. Once we've done it often enough it'll be easy as pie, just you wait and see. You just have to remember to pause if the audience is laughing. No good saying the next bit if they can't hear you.'

I put my head on one side, 'Won't that look odd, just pausing?'

'No, they'll be too busy laughing and you can always pull a face or something. By the way, there was something I meant to tell you.'

'What's that?'

'I was in the Devonshire Arms the other night and I could hear this bloke boasting about robbing things from people's houses. I couldn't see him properly, but I think it was that bloke you know. Your friend's brother.'

'Alun? You mean he's stupid enough to boast about something like that in public?'

'You're not joking. For all he knew, I could have been a policeman. He'd be locked up by now if I was. Didn't you say you and your friend lived near him?'

I nodded, 'Yes, we've got two rooms opposite his girlfriend's. Mind you, he's not there much. I think he's probably got another girl on the go as well. He's such a creep I can't think why anyone would want him.'

David got out his cigarettes and lit one, 'Perhaps they like the stockings and things he gives them.'

'I suppose so, but it'd take a lot more than that for me to go anywhere near him.'

His hand tightened on mine, 'I'm glad to hear that, Lily. You're a very special girl.'

Just then, the music stopped and Freddie, a postman, came on. He was a natural comedian. We stopped to listen.

'I say, I say, I say, have you heard the one about...'.

'My wife's gone mad in Venezuela.'

'Caracas?'

'Yes, blooming nutty.'

'My wife's gone to the Botanic gardens.'

'Kew?'

'Yes, there were rather a lot of people there.'

He had a joke a minute and we laughed so much I got a stitch in my side.

'I hope our audience will like us more after the show.' I said when Freddie had finished.

David paused, 'Well, even if they don't, we've had a good time and I've got to know you better. That's the main thing as far as I'm concerned.'

It was harder and harder to remember Edward. And with David being so kind and attentive it was difficult to keep my thoughts in some sort of order.

When I got back to our rooms Bronwyn was there, curling her hair. 'How did the rehearsals go?' she asked, twisting her hair into a rag roller.

'They were good, Freddie told a lot of good jokes. And David...'

She stopped what she was doing, 'David? What are you going to do about him, Lily? He's been keen on you for a long time.'

'But Edward...'

She pulled a face as she picked up another rag, 'I'm not being funny nor nothing, but I've said it before and I'll say it again. Times are different now. Who knows if Edward will ever come home. Even if he does you may have gone off each other. And any of us could get killed tonight in the bombing. Live while you can, that's what I say.'

I bit my cheek, 'Thing is, Bron, David's not like your married men. He'd want a proper relationship, not a quick bit of how's-your-father.'

She looked at herself in the mirror, checking her rollers were even, 'Sounds like a good one to me.'

'That's the trouble, he is a good one. If Edward comes back, I'd have to let one of them down. That'd be horrible.'

'Sounds to me like you need to keep your knickers on firmly then. When the show is over, you could try to avoid being on duty with him.'

The trouble was, I didn't want to.

Alun often popped into our rooms on some pretext or another, usually to cadge something. Very occasionally he bought a gift of stockings or a tin of spam. We were unprincipled enough to take them.

Then he started asking me about my job. He'd never shown the slightest bit of interest before, but I suppose Bronwyn had told him I worked in a depot. Suddenly he was the world's best listener, asking questions about what was stocked, staff numbers and so on. Of course, I didn't tell him. Even if there hadn't been a war on, I wouldn't have told him, the lazy crook.

Then one day I walked to the bus on my way to work and

just got a feeling I was being followed. It was a chilly day with a cutting wind and everyone was well wrapped up with coats, scarves and hats. That morning there had been ice on the inside of the windows in our room.

I looked round several times but there were always a good number of people nearby and I couldn't see anyone I recognised. Even so, the hairs on my neck stood up and I felt a cold shiver down my spine that wasn't entirely due to the weather.

On the bus I checked to see if someone was following me, but it was standing room only and I couldn't see everyone. Giving myself a good talking-to, I dismissed my feelings as being lack of sleep after yet another night down the air raid shelter. But I was just about to step into the offices when I turned and caught sight of Alun, dodging into one of the warehouses. I could hardly believe my eyes. That man had such cheek. The most surprising thing was that he was up and about that early, usually he didn't get up til the middle of the day. Probably tired after his criminal activities during the bombing every night.

Clenching my jaw, I strode towards the warehouse, but stopped before anyone inside could see me. This could be my chance to find out more about who was stealing stuff. Pulling my coat closer, I tiptoed towards the door and peered in. Alun was talking to one of the men who worked there. But I was disappointed to find the man didn't fit the description I'd been given in the pub after the train crash. I did my best to listen to their conversation, but there was too much noise from the road, the railway and other men working. Then someone in the yard walked by with a cheery 'Good morning, Lily.' and I gave up and went into the office.

That evening Alun appeared at our door; this time he wanted to borrow some bread. The arrogant swagger was back and you'd never know I'd kneed him and thrown him out of our previous rooms. The suit he never seemed to take off was shinier than ever and the collar of his shirt was frayed.

I handed him enough bread for two slices; we couldn't spare more.

'Thanks, Doll,' he said, tipping his hat, 'pay you back some time.'

My top lip curled, 'Yeah, and pigs might fly.'

'Don't be like that, you know I treat you and Bron well. Bring you stuff, don't I?'

I took a deep breath, 'I saw you at the depot earlier. What were you doing there?'

He pulled the ciggie out of his mouth and frowned, 'What d'you mean, at the depot?'

'I saw you, you must have followed me. Don't try to deny it.'

He flicked his ash into a saucer. 'Oh yeah, I forgot, called in to see my mate, needed to talk to him about something.'

I put my hands on my hips, 'What? What did you need to talk about?'

'None of your business. I don't ask you about people you talk to. Keep your nose out of my business or there'll be no more stockings for you.'

And with that, he spun on his heel and walked out.

'You're kidding, I can't do Jean's slot!' I looked at Jim, the variety show organiser, in horror.

He put his arm round my shoulder and gave it a squeeze. 'Come on, Lily, help us out. She's got tonsillitis, poor thing, no way she can sing.'

I pulled myself away from him, 'But I can't sing either, you just ask my mum.'

He laughed, 'Well, your mum's wrong. I've heard you singing along to Jean's song in rehearsals loads of time and you're good.'

'But...' I looked at David for support.

He blew me a kiss, 'He's right, Lily, you can sing that song and you'll be great. Pretend you're singing in the bath.'

'But I don't sing in the bath!'

He went over to the flower arrangement at the side of the stage and took out a daffodil. Then he bowed and handed it to me, 'You'll be a star, Lily, an absolute star.'

Jim stood in front of me and took my hands in his, 'Please, Lily, without Jean's song the show will be shorter. Not only that, but people love a good singalong. It lifts their spirits and God know we could all do with that.'

'That's right, Lily,' David pipped up, 'You just do the first little bit, then encourage them to sing along. They'll love it. Everyone knows Over the Rainbow.'

I scrapped my hand through my hair and glanced at the exit, wondering if I dared run away.

'Please, please, Lily.' Jim said, 'We'll love you forever. Not that we don't already, of course.'

'But what about my sketch with David?'

David took my hand and I was so distracted, I didn't even get a thrill like I normally would. 'That's twenty minute later. You'll have plenty of time to calm down, change your outfit and get ready.'

By now, all the others were crowded round me, 'Go on Lily, you can do it!' 'Save us all!'

'But I've got nothing to wear!' It was my last ditch attempt to get out of singing.

With a flourish Jim reached into his bag and produced a

dress, floor length, deep red with sequins round the neckline. 'Jean says you can wear hers. She was sure you're the same size.'

My shoulders sagged and I looked down at my feet, giving a long sigh, 'Oh, okay, but it's your fault if they throw tomatoes at me!'

Jim slapped me on the back so firmly I almost fell over. The others gave a round of applause, a bit premature because most of them hadn't heard me sing.

'Come on,' David said, indicating a small changing room, 'Let's practice a couple of times, then you can come and try it on the stage before the audience gets here.'

Another ARP warden, Cathy, came with us. I was so nervous, a pathetic squeak was all that happened when I tried to sing.

''ere,' Cathy said, handing me a glass with half a pint of stout, 'That'll give you some hairs on your chest. Think of all the awful things you've seen and dealt with doing ARP. This'll be a doddle compared to that.'

She was right. I drank the half pint in three gulps, then worried it would make my stomach stick out too much in Jean's figure hugging dress. I'd have to try to pee it all out before the performance.

I started to sing, 'Oh, oh, oh, Somewhere...' Cathy stopped me.

'No, get yourself more upright.' She pulled my shoulders back like I was made of plasticine. 'If you hunch your shoulders you'll have no hope of singing loud enough for everyone to hear you. You gotta project your voice.'

My next attempt wasn't much better.

'Imagine you're rolling your voice to the back of the auditorium,' she said, 'that'll do the trick.'

Fifteen minute and a lot of prodding, poking and advice later, she dragged me onto the stage.

'Now, girl, I'm going to sit in them there stalls with David and we want you to sing your 'eart out. Remember to encourage us to join in and we will!'

I waited until they were seated, then gave myself a good talking to. I took a deep breath and decided to pretend I was Jean. She always walked with confidence, her steps firm and upright. 'Stop thinking about yourself,' I muttered, 'think about giving them a good time!'

And with that I stepped forward and sang, so much better than I'd been doing. I bent forward and waved my arm at Cathy and David after the first few lines and they joined in, their smiles wide and encouraging.

There was a burst of applause and I was surprised to find all the other performers had been watching from the wings. I smiled and gave a bow as if they were royalty.

I felt amazing. Powerful. And even more surprising, I found I was looking forward to singing in front of a full audience. Me!

Jean was right, her dress fitted me a treat although I was glad I had my roll-on corset with me. Not that I was having trouble peeing. Nerves made me go every five minutes. I looked in the mirror and didn't recognise myself, I looked quite glamorous. I gave myself a big grin and took the dress off again. Best to put it on at the last minute in case I spilled something down it.

At last it was time. The audience started to file in, and we heard plenty of chatter. 'They should be in a good mood,' Cathy said, 'not often they get a show for free.'

David had gone to the back of the auditorium to help people to their seats and me and the other performers restlessly waited to start, our nervousness showing with strained laughter and fidgeting.

Cathy noticed it first. It was two minutes to curtain up, 'What's going on?' she whispered. We were standing in the wings, listening to people arrive, but the sound had changed. People gradually went quiet.

She pulled the heavy red velvet curtain aside a couple of inches and peered out.

'What is it?' I tried looking over her shoulder.

She let the curtain drop, 'I dunno, but there's something going on right at the back. Everyone's turning round looking at something. Can't see what it is.'

The band were just about to play the music to introduce the start of the show when we heard the whisper murmured by several hundred voices...

'Churchill, it's Churchill.'

Cathy looked at me. 'Bloody hell, they're saying Churchill. We ain't got a Churchill impersonator doing a bit, 'ave we?'

I wrapped my arms around myself, and my stomach seemed to have dropped to the floor. There was no impersonator on the books.

I looked at Cathy, but she just shrugged her shoulders. 'Come on, they're starting.'

'But Churchill...'

She patted my arm, 'Don't be daft, it must just be someone who looks like 'im. He's too busy running a war to come to a little show like this. Come on girl, the band's about to start.'

Of course, of course, I told myself, she's right. My shoulders relaxed and I took three deep breaths.

I waited until the curtains had opened and Jim said, 'Good afternoon, Ladies and Gentlemen,' then I went backstage to put on Jean's dress. I wasn't on for fifteen minutes so I had time to put on the make-up, remembering Cathy's advice to put on a lot more than usual. When I'd finished, I turned to the other girls who were in various stages of getting ready. 'Does this look okay or do I look tarty?'

One of them stopped and looked at me, 'You look bloody gorgeous my love, just go out there and wow them like you did before.'

I looked at the clock. Time to go to the wings and wait for my call. I peeked out at the audience who were watching a dance routine. They were good as gold, and the atmosphere felt friendly. *Nothing to worry about* I told myself, *just help them forget the Blitz for a few minutes and have a good sing-song.*

Then, the music stopped, the dancers finished. As they walked past me they smiled and someone said, 'Break a leg.'

There was a drum roll, and Jim was standing there, his arm out waiting for me to go on stage. In my terror I hadn't even heard him introducing me.

It was the first time I'd been on stage with a full audience and lights shining in my face. Jim saw me hesitate and jokingly escorted me to the middle of the stage 'Come on, everyone, give the lovely Lily a big round of applause!'

Bless him! I unfroze my face and smiled and him, took a step closer to the microphone and then the music started

The song went so quickly I couldn't remember it afterwards. I've heard people say the same thing about their weddings. But the audience sang along and I got another round of applause when I'd finished so it must have been good enough.

When I walked off stage David was waiting in the wings, a huge smile one his face. He grabbed me and twirled me round, 'You're a star,' he said, 'they loved you.' He put me down and took a step back, 'But now you've got to get ready for our stint.'

After my solo singing, our short comedy sketch seemed easy, although I still got butterflies in my stomach and a dry mouth until we'd said the first few lines. Jim's gags got several laughs. When we left the stage, I was elated. Two performances, doing things I'd never done before, and I wondered if I could find time to join an amateur dramatics group if any were still operating.

When the show had finished, we had a party in The King's Head nearby. The landlord had kept a good space for us and we were high with success. Jim produced a bottle of bubbly. There was only enough for half a glass each but it made us feel very special.

Jim tapped his glass and stood on a chair, 'Ladies and gentlemen, thespians, I raise my glass to you. You put on a terrific show, every single act a winner. I listened to people as they left and I can tell you they were very happy.'

'Will it stop them moaning when we remind them about the black-out?' someone shouted.

Jim grinned, 'I don't suppose it will, but you never know, you might just get the odd cup of tea or something.'

'Was that Churchill sitting in the back?' I asked him. He looked at David.

They shrugged, 'It certainly looked like him, and there were a couple of burly blokes with him. Could have been body-guards. Maybe he wanted to see a bit of real life.'

'And maybe it was a look-alike messing about.' David said, 'We'll never know because he never said a word and left before the end.'

When David went to the bar to buy more drinks Cathy nudged me, 'You and David an item then?' she asked.

I caught my breath, not knowing how to answer. Were

we? Had I given up on Edward? The guilt that usually strangled me when I tried to think this through was short lived, probably because I was feeling a bit squiffy.

'There's not really time to go home before our shift,' I said to David as we left the pub and our fellow thespians behind. We were still feeling euphoric about the success of our show and I couldn't speak for David, but I felt like skipping down the road.

It was mid afternoon and a chilly day. Low clouds, grey as an old man's beard, hung motionless in the sky. I pulled my scarf tighter round my neck and put on the gloves I found amongst the clothes donated for people who'd been bombed out. Whoever knitted them must have used leftover balls of wall, they were stripes of every colour under the sun.

David saw me shiver and took my hand in his, glove to glove. He pulled me closer and we walked in silence through the fading afternoon. I wished it was warm enough for us to hold hands skin to skin.

'We've got a couple of hours before we're on duty,' he said helping me round a pile of bricks from a damaged house, 'Better not have any more alcohol or we'll be useless doing our ARP duties. But I live near here. If you like, I've got tea and some crumpets we could toast.'

I paused, my heart beating fast, 'And, let me guess, you'd like to show me your etchings?'

He stopped briefly and looked at me, smiling. 'Damn, I forgot to do any. But I've got some nice books. Will they do?'

'Maybe, what sort are they? Do they have pictures?'

He squeezed my hand, 'If they don't, I'll draw some for you.'

'Gosh, another one of your talents.'

He squeezed my hand, 'I've got many more if you'd let me show you.'

I realised we were flirting more than we'd let ourselves do in the past. I couldn't believe how forward I'd been and suddenly lost my nerve. 'A cup of tea and a crumpet would be lovely.'

His rooms were luxurious compared to mine and Bronwyn's. He had a bedroom, kitchen/living room and his own tiny bathroom. I looked around and guessed he'd lived there with his late wife. A woman's touch was here and there with a little vase on the mantlepiece and lace antimacassars on the back of the small sofa and armchair. The curtains were cream with pink and red flowers.

I walked over to his bookshelf. I've always thought you can tell a lot about people by the books they read. I grew up in a house where books were a rarity and I still think of them as a luxury. David had a bookcase full. I read the titles, *Down and out in Paris and London* by George Orwell, *Brave new world* by Aldous Huxley. Serious stuff. I'd only read the Huxley one. Then I spotted *The Code of the Woosters*, by P.G. Woodhouse and a few Agatha Christy. If I didn't already believe it, his selection convinced me we had plenty in common.

He saw be looking, 'Borrow any of them if you like,' he said, 'Let me light the fire and then I'll put the kettle on the ring and we can toast the crumpets,' David said.

I watched as he laid the fire; the careful way he placed the crumpled newspaper, then the wooden sticks and finally the coal. As he lit the paper the flames reflected on the fine hairs on the back of his hands and on the thick fair hair on his head. He sat back on his heels and held his hand out for me to help him up even though he was more than capable of standing without my help.

He stood and took my other hand in his, looking into my face without speaking, a small smile curving the corners of his mouth. Then, as if remembering himself he said, 'Oh my goodness, I've got coal dust all over your hands. You go to the bathroom to wash them while I put the kettle on.'

My pulse, lifted up by the feel of his hands, calmed as I washed mine. I looked in the mirror. Was I ready for whatever happened next? I could almost hear Bronwyn cheering me on. *Go on, you silly girl,* she'd say, *you could be dead tomorrow. Have a bit of fun.*

I ran my fingers through my hair, then undid the top button on my high-necked blouse, though it was still far from revealing. It was cold in that bathroom but I could feel a hot flush rising up by body and took some deep breaths before going back to join David. He was spooning tea leaves in a brown pot and had laid two delicate cups and saucers on a little table along with a china milk jug and sugar bowl. The fire was beginning to draw and I sat on the sofa finally feeling warm enough to take off my coat.

He came and sat next to me, our legs touching on the small sofa. 'Here,' he said, handing me the toasting fork, 'you can do the first crumpet.' He stood up again and fetched some butter and jam then joined me again. The fire burned red and gold, tiny golden sparks catapulting in all directions. It smelled of wood and coal and bought happy Christmas mornings to my mind.

'Let me turn that over. First crumpet's for you.' David said, taking the fork from me.

But I waited for his to be ready and we bit into them at the same time, eyes locked, precious butter making our lips glisten. We smiled at each other then jumped as the fire crackled and roared like distant thunder. A spark landed on the rug and he jumped up to stamp it out. The crumpet tasted heavenly, although whether it was the treat of butter and jam or the company I wasn't sure. When we'd finished eating David took my hand, 'Lily, you must know how I feel about you...'

I blushed and nodded, not knowing how to answer.

'You know I've been married... and you...'

I gave a tiny shake of my head then took a deep breath, stood up and led him towards the bedroom. The room was simple. A double bed with a blue candlewick bedspread and the same curtains as the living room. A wardrobe and dressing table stood along one wall. It was cold after sitting by the fire and he stopped to light an electric fire in the small grate. The dusty smell it gave off showed he rarely allowed himself the treat of a warm bedroom.

He turned back to me, a question in his eyes, 'Lily, are you sure...'

I nodded and sat on the bed, 'I don't know what to do, David. You'll have to show me.' I said, my voice trembling.

He sat beside me and rubbed my hands between his. Then he turned one over and kissed my palm gently. 'I've only... you know... with my wife... so... well, we can learn together.'

He started to unbutton my cardigan and I was surprised that his hands were shaking. I giggled, 'We're as daft as each other.' I said, and undid the buttons on his shirt, then tentatively stroked his chest, with its light covering of fair hair. 'I've never felt a man's chest before,' I said, 'well, not one who was alive anyway.'

He grinned, 'When I think of the body parts we...'

I put my finger to his lips, 'Let's not talk about horrible things now.'

He leaned toward me and kissed me, gently and then with

passion. His kisses, softer than a feather yet stronger than iron, left me breathless and wanting more. His hands, warmer now, found their way inside my blouse and vest and he cupped his hands over my breasts through my cotton bra.

'I've never been any good at undoing those things,' he said, 'you're going to have to help me.'

Although the electric fire was helping, the room was still a bit too cold.

'Tell you what,' I said, 'let's get undressed and get in bed. But don't look!'

He laughed, 'Don't you look either then!'

I didn't dare strip off completely and jumped into bed still wearing my bra and knickers. I pulled the covers up to my chin like a little child listening to a bedtime story, and then watched as he jumped in, still wearing his underpants.

'Not a very brave pair, are we.' I said, grinning.

'Blimey, these sheets are cold,' he said, 'better cuddle up or we'll freeze to death.'

His arm around me felt safe and strong and the masculine smell of him was something I knew I'd never forget. A car back-fired down in the street, making us both look at the window. A bird was on the sill, chirping to its mate. 'He looks happy,' I said, 'but not as happy as me.'

'Not as happy as me either,' he replied, 'you have no idea how long I'd hoped this would happen. You're a very special person, Lily, and a singing star as well.'

I starting humming *Over the rainbow,* but he stopped me with another kiss and this time, he managed to undo all the fasteners on my bra. He tasted of tea and butter and himself. He stroked my breast then paused, 'Are you sure you're sure?'

In response, I put my hand on his chest again. 'I'll tell you if I want you to stop. Just be gentle.'

I knew I didn't need to say that. David seemed incapable

of being anything but considerate.

A sudden squall of rain battered the windows and distracted us, but only for a second. Soon we were beyond hearing anything but each other; beyond smelling anything but the scent of our emotions; beyond feeling anything but skin; soft, giving, hard, yielding; beyond hearing anything but our gasps and whispered endearments.

~

It hurt a little, as I expected, but only for a second, and David was kindness itself. The brief pain was soon forgotten in the pleasure of our love-making. I'd always thought that sex would be hurried and silent, but we talked, we laughed, we stroked, we coupled, we loved. I looked at David, wondering how he felt about me. I'd always been told that men didn't respect girls who 'did it' before marriage, yet I instinctively felt this wouldn't be true for him. But I still needed reassurance.

'David... I...' I couldn't look him in the eye.

He leaned forward and kissed me once more, 'I think I love you, Lily. I'm so glad we're on duty together tonight. We don't have to say goodbye yet.'

My shoulders relaxed and I started to dress. Did I love David? I wasn't sure. My feelings for him were different from those I felt for Edward. But were either love? I had no idea how to tell, but I knew that I wanted to spend a lot of time with this wonderful man finding out.

'Lily, there's something I must tell you,' he started, then another squall of rain finally bought us back to reality and we looked at the clock and realised we only had a short time before we were on duty. 'I'll tell you another time.' he said reaching for his clothes.

Bronwyn came in, smelling of winter, her face red raw from riding the motor bike.

'Get the kettle on, I'm as cold as a dog's nose.' she said, taking off her coat and grabbing a dressing gown to put over her clothes.

'Come and warm your hands by the fire. Want some toast?' I'd made the fire up and it crackled cheerfully in the grate. I headed to our food store and took out the remains of a loaf. It was a bit stale, but fine toasted.

She sat down, hands outstretched to the heat. 'Do you ever dream about the days when we could have toast dripping with butter? None of this bloody rationing.'

I scraped the butter on her toast, and scraped off the excess, although before the war no-one would have thought it was excessive. 'I dream about that, and being about to buy clothes without coupons, about not being terrified of bombs every night...'

She took the toast and looked at me for the first time. 'Hey, you look different...' she took a bite and looked harder as she chewed, 'you've got a sort of glow...'

'Sitting by the fire too much, I suppose.' I said, trying to head her off.

She suddenly stood, 'I've got it!' she slapped her hands together, almost dropping her toast, 'You've done it, haven't you!'

I busied myself putting the bread away. She turned me round abruptly and looked closely at my face.

'Yes, I'm right. You've only gone and lost your bloody cherry, haven't you!'

I smiled and said nothing.

A frown creased her lovely face, 'But what about Edward?

Remember him? Your fiancé? The one you were going to wait for for ever.'

My mouth dropped open, 'But you said... you said I should enjoy myself... I could be dead tomorrow.'

'I never thought you'd damn well do it though, did I? Miss Goody Shoes like you, I thought you'd wait til you knew for sure about Edward.'

My body tensed and my breathing was shallow. 'How dare you! You and your married men! And you think you've got a right to criticise me, you hypocrite. You have no idea how lonely I've been.'

Her lip curled, 'So you had sex just cos you were lonely, did you? You should have got yourself a teddy bear.'

'It's not just that. David's...'

'Lovely... I know, you've told me often enough. But still, Edward...'

I sat down heavily, my eyes filling with tears, 'Edward's been missing such a long time. Surely if he was alive I'd have heard something. He's not on the prisoner-of-war lists and...'

She folded her arms, 'And you've done nothing to try to find out more. Ever thought about going to his regiment?'

I sobbed, 'But if they knew anything they'd...'

'Have told you. Or that wretched mother of his. But what about his mates? The ones he was with. Some of them might have come back. Go and find them and see if they know anything. Better than moping about.'

I looked up, 'I wasn't moping. I was quite happy 'til you came in.'

'Well, you should be sitting there feeling bloody guilty.'

I took a deep breath, 'What, like you, you mean? Going out with married men? Taking gifts off them like a...'

She glared at me, 'A what...?'

'Nothing,' I suddenly felt deflated as a punctured tyre,

'let's not argue, Bron. So we're not angels, neither of us, but we can still be friends. Come on, we've been through so much together.'

She sat back down and took the last bite of her toast. I thought she'd sulk for ever so was glad when the landlord knocked on the door for his rent. By the time he'd had a chat and we'd batted away his attempts to get fresh with us, our argument was forgotten.

'Do you really think it would do any good going to Edward's regiment?' I said when we'd settled down again.

She shrugged, 'It's like this, see, I don't know. But it can't do any harm trying, can it? Want me to come with you?'

~

Three days later we headed for the Regiment's head quarters, dressed in our uniforms in the hope that we would get more response than if we were in our civvies. We polished our shoes and badges to a shine; no point in having some picky officer using it as an excuse to look down his nose at us.

The train and then bus to the HQ seemed to take for ever and I was glad we'd made a prompt start even though it meant getting up early after spending half the night in the air raid shelter.

'Are you sure it's a good idea going without making an appointment?' I asked Bronwyn, butterflies fighting for space in my stomach.

She nodded, 'Like I said, if we make an appointment, they can make it months ahead, put us off like. If this way doesn't work, we can always make an appointment.'

'You girls going to the army head quarters?' an old soldier

with one arm missing asked us, 'sorry to be nosy but I couldn't help overhearing you.'

I turned to him, 'Yes, my fiancé is missing presumed dead and I want to know if they know any more than they've told us.'

He took off his hat and scratched his head, then put his hat back on again. 'That's a tough one, for sure. They'll only tell you what they know officially. If you don't get any joy from them there officers, try talking to the blokes in his battalion. Some of them'll at least know the gossip. Some of them might have even seen something. You'll have to be cunning though. Them officers'll try to get you out of the compound as soon as they can.'

My heart sank, 'Are they all difficult?'

He shook his head, 'Some of 'em are okay, but others think they're above talking to ordinary people, even girls in uniform like you two.'

The bus dropped us right outside and we stood and gazed at the entrance without moving. I looked at Bronwyn, she seemed as unsure as me but I shrugged, put my arm through hers, and stepped forward wondering what was to come.

A soldier holding a rifle stopped us getting through the gate. He'd been standing inside a sentry box and stepped out calling 'Halt!'

I swallowed hard, 'We want to see someone about my fiancé who's missing in action.' I said, trying not to let the tears that threatened to roll down my cheeks.

His expression turned from formal to sympathetic. 'Oh, I see. See the green hut over there?' he pointed over to the left, 'Ask for Captain Smithers, he's the man who deals with that sort of thing. Good luck.'

We had to knock three times before we heard a terse 'Enter!'

Captain Smithers was sitting behind a desk. It was chaotic, like someone had thrown the contents of a filing cabinet in the air and it had all landed on his desk and been left there. My head felt woolly just looking at it and I wondered how he could possibly work efficiently in that muddle. He was in uniform of course, but somehow managed to make it look scruffy. There was dandruff on his collar and his tie was slightly crooked. Another soldier, not an officer, sat at a desk nearby. His desk was the opposite. Two metal wire trays held papers, but apart from that the only things on his desk were the paper he was working on, a typewriter and two pens. The room smelled of cigarette smoke and dust.

Captain Smithers looked up. 'Oh!' he said, 'girls! Not at all what I was expecting. What are you doing here?'

We stepped forward but he didn't invite us to sit in the chair in front of his desk. 'Good morning Captain Withers, I'm Lily Baker and this is my friend Bronwyn Jones. My fiancé has been reported missing in action ages ago and I wondered if there is any more news.'

He blinked several times, 'Have you made an appointment to see me?'

'No, we hoped it would be okay to come without an appointment.'

He sighed, 'What's his name?'

'Edward Halpen.'

'Battalion?'

I told him.

He shook his head, 'I can tell you now, there's no more news. Do you have any idea how many men have gone missing? We have great responsibility here. We tell families everything we know as soon as we know it. You're wasting your time here, I'm afraid.'

With that, he waved us away and started shuffling papers. The man at the other desk just looked up and gave a sympathetic half smile.

'If we make an appointment, would you have more time to check?' Bronwyn said, ignoring his attempt to get rid of us.

He looked up, a pained expression on his face, 'No, I think I've explained that we tell families all we know as soon as we know it. I'm sorry but I can't help you any further. I'm afraid I must get on now.'

Back at the gate, the guard saw our down-cast faces. 'No luck, ladies?'

I shook my head, 'No, he couldn't help.'

He looked around as if checking there was no-one who could overhear. 'What battalion are we talking about here?'

He thought when I told him, his lips pursed, 'Tell you what, go and speak to Corporal Johnson.' he looked at his watch, 'If you're lucky he'll just be knocking off and heading for the mess for a bite to eat.' He indicated a green hut to the right, further away than Captain Smither's one. 'Try in there, but whatever you do, don't say I told you. They'll have my guts for garters!'

We scurried to the hut expecting to be challenged any minute, but apart from the odd wolf-whistle no-one took any notice of us. We knocked on the door and there was an immediate response to come in.

Corporal Johnson was tidying his desk. He looked up, then blinked rapidly when he saw us, 'Good day, young ladies. Who did you want to see?'

I was relieved that he seemed more friendly than Captain Smithers. 'We're here to see Corporal Johnson.'

'Well, you've found him, Sweetheart. What can I do for you?' His stomach rumbled and he patted it distractedly.

I was reminded how little I knew about what Edward had

been doing before he went missing. We were so well trained not to tell anyone anything *Walls have ears* that we deliberately didn't ask questions. We talked about people we worked with and other things about everyday life, but not what we were doing day to day in the military. I didn't even know what country Edward was in when he went missing.

All this meant that it didn't take long to tell Corporal Johnson all I knew. He listened seriously, his face kind. 'I don't know anything myself,' he said, 'and it's likely that you've been told all there is to know. In the horrible muddle of war it's not surprising that information is hard to come by.'

My face dropped and I shuffled my feet, 'Do you think there is anyone who would know?' My voice shook as I asked.

He paused for a minute, 'Well, love, I can't tell you anything that's classified information. You're in uniform, you understand that. And I don't know anything myself. But tell you what, I'll ask around and see if I can find out anything. You'll need to give me a few days though. Why not come back a week today. I'll be on duty all day. How would that be?'

I could have kissed him. Instead, I smiled broadly and thanked him, then Bronwyn and I said goodbye and headed out of the camp.

'Have you thought how you'll feel if it seems pretty certain Edward is dead?' she asked as we waited at the bus stop opposite the camp.

I got my money ready, looking down the road in case the bus came, 'I've thought of nothing else since he went missing.'

'Yes, but it's different now. There's David. You'll feel...'

I sighed, 'Guilty. That's me, guilty if Edward is dead,

guilty if he's alive. I wish I'd never listened to you and all your talk about living for the moment.'

She laughed, 'You're not still blaming me, are you? I don't think what I said had anything to do with it. You two were going to get together without my say-so.'

The bus arrived and it saved me from having to say she was right.

And I would be seeing David again that evening on ARP duty. Little could I know what would happen.

'Her pulse all right? Damn, her head's started bleeding again.' The man's voice was far away as if I was dreaming. Someone replied but I couldn't hear what they said, my ears buzzed too much. A hand pressed something against my head.

I'm not in my bed, I thought, *what's happening?* I struggled to open my heavy eyes and saw a white wall next to me with writing on it, but I couldn't make sense of the letters. My brain felt filled with fog and the letters swam in front of me. I became aware of pain in my head and my left arm. The more I woke up, the worse the pain got. I moved a little and groaned.

'Thank God, she's coming round again.' the voice said. A face peered into mine, 'You've been injured in a bomb blast love, we're taking you to the hospital.'

The words meant nothing, it was as though they were speaking in a foreign language under water.

'What's your name, Love?' the voice said. I didn't understand the question.

He shook my shoulder gently, 'I said, what's your name, Love?'

I understood the question but had no idea who I was. Suddenly I realised that whatever I was in was moving and felt sick. My eyes widened.

'You're in an ambulance, Love.' the voice said, 'we're taking you to hospital. The hospital. Do you remember us telling you before?'

'Before?' my voice seemed to belong to someone else.

'Don't worry about it, Love. You've had a bang in the head, makes you forget things. You'll be fine, just got to sort out that arm of yours.'

I went to shake my head in an attempt to clear it, but it hurt too much. 'Keep still, now.' he said, 'That cut on your head is going to need a few stitches. The doc will do that in no time, you'll be as good as new.'

He gently held my face in his hands to make sure I understood. 'Where am I?' I asked, my mouth dry as sandpaper.

'You're in an ambulance and we're taking you to hospital. You've been in a bomb blast.'

'I need... I need...' I wriggled by lower half.

'You need to spend a penny? We've got bedpan here.' He vanished briefly, then came back carrying something, 'Can you do this? I can help you but most ladies don't like us pulling down their drawers if you get my drift.'

Still feeling as if I were detached from reality, I wriggled my knickers down, not easy with one hand and the other arm hurting like hell. He pushed the bedpan under me. A strategically placed sheet saved my embarrassment. Peeing lying down was a strange experience and added to my sense of confusion.

He'd just taken the bedpan from me when the ambulance - I now understood where I was - slowed down. 'We're here, love, St. George's. Soon have you better.'

The next time I was properly taking things in, I was in

bed in a crowded ward, beds so close together the nurses could barely walk between us. I looked around at the other patients. They all slept or had bandages or plaster casts, one or two groaned in pain. I'd drifted in and out of consciousness while the doctors did x-rays and stitched my head. I put up my hand to feel the big bandage on my head, but my hand was heavy because of the plaster on my arm.

A doctor stopped at the end of my bed, 'How are you feeling now, Miss Baker? Can you remember what happened?'

'What...? Where...?

He looked down at my chart. 'You were on ARP duty and got caught in a bomb blast. You're one of the lucky ones, you've had concussion, that's why your head hurts. You'll probably have a headache for a few days, but it looks like you'll make a full recovery.'

When he left I struggled to remember what happened. I remembered walking down the road with David, then the alarm going. That was it. Nothing else until I was in the ambulance, and that was hazy as if someone was snatching the memory away from me every time I went near it.

I slept again and when I woke up Bronwyn was sitting by my bed, a frown creasing her brow. She smiled when I looked at her, 'Thank goodness. I worried you'd never wake up. How are you, Lily?'

I tried to sit up but between my thumping head and broken arm couldn't do it. A nurse walking by helped Bronwyn and they put some pillows behind me so I was upright.

'I still can't remember much, Bronwyn. How did they know to tell you I was here?' I was relieved that my brain was a bit clearer.

She held my hand, 'The ARP people came round. You'd put me down as next of kin. Local, anyway.'

I blinked and was surprised to find tears filling my eyes, 'What about Mum?'

She nodded, 'I've sent her a telegram. She sent one back and said she'll be here tomorrow morning. She said you're to stay with her 'til you're better.'

She took my hand in hers, ‘Do you remember what happened?'

I fiddled with my sheet with my good hand, 'When I was injured? I keep getting sort of glimpses, but they vanish before I can get hold of them.'

We were interrupted by a nurse pushing a thermometer in my mouth and grabbing my wrist to take my pulse. 'How're you two girls,' she said, 'catching up with news?'

Before we had chance to answer she was gone, on to the next patient.

Bronwyn looked at the clock, and I noticed for the first time that she was in uniform, 'I'm so sorry, Cariad, but I've got to go. I'm on duty. But I'll come and see you tomorrow. Don't go rushing off to Oxford without letting me know.'

I barely replied before drifting off to sleep again.

I woke up two hours later to find Jim sitting by my bedside. He was the head of our ARP section and the variety show organiser. He had his cloth cap in his hands, wringing it as if it was wet through. I looked at him and wondered how many other people might have sat patiently waiting for me to wake up.

'Jim,' I said, my mouth suddenly dry. 'Water.'

He leaned over to my bedside cabinet and poured me a glass. 'How are you doing, Sweetheart?'

I drank several sips and handed the glass back to him. 'Jim, I can't remember what happened. Do you know?'

His face dropped and he bit his lip, 'I do, love. You know

you were on duty. You and David had seen people into the shelters when the alarms went off, then you were doing the blackouts check.'

'I don't remember any of that.'

He patted my hand, 'They say it's not unusual to forget things that happen before a bang on the head.'

'The doctor said I'd been injured in a bomb blast. David was with me on duty, wasn't he? I'm sure I remember that. How is he? Is he in this hospital?'

'The all-clear had just gone off when another bomb dropped. We think it was a Jerry on the way back wanted to get rid of his last bomb. Lucky people hadn't come out of the shelter yet.'

I held my breath, he hadn't answered my question. 'But David, what about David?'

'I'm so sorry, Love, it's not good news.'

I clutched my sheet. I barely dared look at Jim, 'David, is he... is he...'

He took my hand in his and shook his head, 'I'm sorry Love, I know you were a bit fond of him. Anyone could see that. But he didn't make it.'

'You mean he's...'

'Gone. Yes, I'm so sorry. But it would have been so quick, he wouldn't have suffered and that's a bit of comfort.'

I gasped, feeling as if someone had punched me in the stomach. 'But he can't be... I... We...'

Jim squeezed my hand harder, 'He's gone, Love, there's no mistake. It's a lot to take in, I know, especially when you're feeling so rough yourself.'

I looked down at my bed, feeling numb. Both the men in my life, dead. I'd given up hope that Edward was safe. Was I some sort of jinx on them? Was it my fault in some way?

Jim interrupted my gloomy thoughts, 'I'm really sorry to give you such awful news and go, but I need to get myself organised for tonight. You get properly better before you think about coming back on duty, my dear. Oh, and I saw your boss from the depot on the way in. He'd hoped to see you but you were sleeping and he didn't want to disturb you. He said take as much time as you need to recover. Just let him know when you'll be back at work when you know.'

He bent down and picked up a bar of chocolate which he gave me awkwardly. 'Not much of a compensation, this, but you'll know that we all care for you when you eat it.'

'But David...'

The corners of his mouth drooped, 'You'll be wanting to know about his funeral, I expect. Let me know where you are when you leave here and I'll make sure you're told. I can escort you there if you'd like me to.'

I got very little sleep that night and when I did my dreams were nightmares: bombs, screaming, David, Edward, all mixed together in a way that woke me feeling fractured.

Mum was first through the door at visiting time next day. Her smile was mixed with worry, 'Oh Lily,' she said, kissing me on the cheek, 'I've been so worried about you. How are you?'

She put a small bag of sweets in my hand. They were so hard to come by she must have gone to a lot of effort to get it.

'I'm okay,' I said, and could hear the break in my voice, 'my head is a lot clearer now.'

She sat down and held my hand. 'What happened? I only know what your friend Bronwyn said in her telegram.'

My breath caught in my throat, 'I was on ARP duty and got caught in the bomb blast. I was with ....' Tears rolled down my cheeks and I sobbed so loudly the visitor at the next bed turned to see what was happening. Once I started it seemed I'd never stop. Mum just sat holding my hand and waiting for me to calm myself.

When I got control she asked, 'What is it, Love, do you want to talk about it?'

I shook my head, 'I can't. Not now.'

Her face dropped, 'Will you come and stay with me while you recover? I wish you would. We have so much making up to do.'

My eyes narrowed, ‘You’re not back with that awful bloke are you?’

'No. I told you, you were right about him all along. He's gone and good riddance.’

It was strange to be back at my old home. Mum's home. She hadn't changed anything in my bedroom. My old books and soft toys were there; the same sheets and candlewick bedspread. The same view out of the window, although now the garden was turned over to vegetables. I was glad she'd managed to plant a few flowers in between them. She'd even got a small chicken run with a couple of chickens who she'd called Hitler and Churchill because they were always pecking at each other.

She kept treating me as if I was made of glass, and it got irritating after the first couple of days. *You sit there and don't do a thing. Have you eaten properly? What can I get you?* My broken arm didn't hurt so much once it was plastered and my head felt a bit better every day, although I still had a dull headache much of the time. It was a relief that she had to go to work and often do overtime. 'Got to make sure the soldiers don't run out of our armaments, haven't we?' she said by way of apology.

I was left alone for long periods so was thrilled when my old friend Jean called the first weekend. We used to work together in a shirt factory and do some shifts in The Dream Palace. Although our jobs had led us both to live in London, work meant that we rarely saw each other. She looked just the same as ever, although she had dark rings round her eyes from lack of sleep. But then, so did everyone who lived in London.

'I got a couple of days leave from the 'ospital,' she said, looking at my head without invitation, ''ow's this wound going?'

I brushed her hand away, 'Stop being a nurse for a minute and sit and chat. I'm alright, really.'

She put the kettle on, 'You been out yet?' she asked over the sound of cups and saucers being put on the tray.

'I've been going for a short walk each day, and I'm getting stronger. I've decided to go back to London in a couple of days.'

She stopped and looked at me, 'If you're okay, why do you still look so done in?'

'Bring the tea in and I'll tell you.' I could hear the weariness in my voice and so could she.

She listened without saying a word for a good five minutes when I told her all about David. 'Well,' she said, handing me a cup, 'you've had a rough time and no mistake. So you fell for this bloke and the poor sod died when you was both on duty. Thank goodness you were safe.'

I hung my head, 'The thing is, Jean, you know I'm engaged to Edward, but me and David, we...'

To my surprise she clapped her hands together, 'You got it together?' I nodded, 'Good for you. So you made some of this David's last memories happy.'

I looked up, 'I hadn't thought of it that way.' I spoke slowly, 'he was happy when we... you know...'

'And I bet ‘e was happy every time he saw you.' she said.

I smiled and it almost hurt, my face had almost forgotten how. 'Yes, we always found something to joke about.'

'Well then, it's wonderful to think how you made his last days and weeks so good. We'd all want that.'

Strangely her words did bring me a little comfort, a ray of hope in the darkness of my gloomy thoughts. 'But what about Edward? He might still come back.'

She sipped her tea, 'He might and then you'll have to decide whether to tell him.'

I could feel my face going red, 'But won't he be able to, you know, tell once we get married?'

She gave a little laugh, 'You daft sod. Not all women are the same. Some bleed a little bit, some not at all. Some hurt, some don't. Take my word for it, you don't need to worry on that account. And there's no need to blush, you daft thing. I'm a nurse, seen and ‘eard everything, trust me.'

This was all news to me. 'That's something, I suppose, but I've got David's funeral tomorrow and I don't know how I'm going to get through it. I've got so many different feelings going round in my head, I can hardly think straight. I'm even angry with him for dying.'

Jean patted my hand, 'Now you listen to me, Lily. I've been nursing long enough to be around a lot of people who've had someone die. Being angry with them for dying is pretty common. I expect you're angry with that awful man Hitler, too. I would be.'

I could only nod as the tears rolled down my cheeks. 'But I miss him so much.' I heard my voice sound childlike as I spoke.

She sat back and folded her arms, 'You missed Edward at first, didn't you? Bet you can ‘ardly remember what he looks like now, can you?'

Her no-nonsense tone book me aback. I'd been expecting sympathy.

'Don't look at me like that,' she said, 'I know you think I'm being harsh but if you'd seen what I see every day on duty...'

I could feel anger rising in my chest, 'But my ARP work...'

'Yes,' she interrupted, 'you saw some awful things. But I see babies dying with measles, mum's dying in childbirth, people dying with all sorts of awful diseases we should be able to cure by now. And all the bomb injured as well. Trust me, Lily, this is awful for you, but in a year you will ‘ave moved on. It's a luxury a lot of people, including your David, won't ‘ave. He'd want you to live your life and be 'appy, wouldn't ‘e! Now, get off that sofa, we're going to the flicks. There's a comedy on and that's just what you need.'

It seemed wrong to laugh when David was dead, but we did. We went to see *The Frozen Limits* and who wouldn't laugh at The Crazy Gang. We laughed until tears rolled down our cheeks. Jean was right, it was just what I needed. Her too, her work was tough day in and day out.

'Would you like me to come to the funeral with you?' she asked as we walked back.

I stopped and looked at her, 'Oh, Jean, would you? It would be so wonderful if you were there, but honestly it's too much to ask.'

She linked her arm through mine, 'It's in London, is it?'

I nodded.

'Well, I've got to be back there tomorrow night ready for

duty next morning, so it's no problem. We can fit some other things in beside the funeral. Are you planning to go to the wake afterwards?'

I frowned and pinched my bottom lip, 'Well, it's probably best if I don't. I won't know anyone there apart from the ARP people. David's mum is dead and his dad is very elderly. I've never met him.'

'Well, it's settled then. I'll make sure you're okay to travel back to your digs on your own what with your ‘ead injury and all. If I'm not convinced I'll put you on a train back to Oxford and your mum.'

Jean was such a tonic, she took me out of myself and made me think life might be okay again. I loved spending time with Mum, but now I was feeling a bit better, I was keen to get back to real life. Even if real life meant life without the two men in my life.

By the time I got back Mum was in and she rushed toward me as I walked in the door.

'Where have you been? I've been so worried about you? Are you okay?'

I took a deep breath and smiled. She only fussed because she loved me. 'I'm fine. Just been to see a film with Jean.'

Before I had time to take my coat off there was a knock on the door. Mum looked at me, 'Who's that then? Are you expecting anyone?'

I shook my head and went to open the door. What I saw made me freeze.

My Dad.

Dad who had walked out ages before to live with his new woman. Dad who'd never bothered to keep in touch with even birthday or Christmas cards. Dad who'd never given Mum a penny.

I kept my hand on the door, it stopped my hand from shaking, 'What do you want?'

He tried to smile but his lips got stuck on his teeth. They were brown from nicotine, just like his fingers. 'I've come to see your mum, love, ain't you going to let me in?'

I held up a hand. 'Wait!'

I slammed the door in his face and hurried into the kitchen. 'Mum, it's Dad, he says he wants to speak to you.'

Her jaw fell open and she dropped the cup she was drying. The sound of it breaking was like a bomb going off. Or maybe that was the state our nerves were in.

She got the dustpan and brush out from under the sink and began clearing up the broken cup, 'Well, I'll talk to him, but you can bet your life he's after something. He's getting nothing out of me. Nothing!'

She walked to the front door, me trailing behind her. She opened it and stood there, her face expressionless. 'What do you want?'

Dad tried that smile again, 'I want to see you, Sweetheart. Ain't you going to invite me in?'

'Give me one good reason why I should.'

He looked down at the ground, 'I've been called up, I wanted to see you both before I go. I might never come back.'

Mum and I stood there for a minute without moving. Like me, she was probably wondering if his story was a pack of lies. Dad reached into his pocket and produced a letter. He took it out of the envelop and held it up for us to see. Sure enough it was his call-up details.

Mum opened the door and stood aside, 'I suppose you'd better come in then, but you're not staying long and we don't have enough tea to feed you.'

'I wouldn't expect you too, Love. It's hard times for everyone.'

He walked in like he'd never been away, looking round at the small changes we'd made. He took his hat off and put it on the table. I noticed for the first time that he looked haggard, and his collar was grubby and his shoes need a clean.

'Sit down,' Mum said, indicating a kitchen chair. She turned to put on the kettle.

I sat opposite him, 'I think this is a pack of lies. You're too old for the draft.'

'I'm not. They've just extended the age to forty one. That's how old I am.'

'Don't be silly, you can't be.' It seemed to me my Dad had always been an old man. His attitudes made him seem older than his bald head and soft belly. He often felt more like a grandfather than a dad. I did the maths. He'd have had to be a very young man when he fathered me.

I was suddenly aware that Mum had gone very still. Dad glanced at her and I turned round so I could see her too. She was blushing so much it was like she was going to have a stroke.

That old saying about cutting the atmosphere with a knife popped into my head. 'What? What's going on?' I looked from one to the other, totally baffled. What did this have to do with Dad being called up?

'Well, it's like this see,' he said, tugging at one ear, 'me and your Mum, well, we were a bit previous, if you get my drift.'

'Previous? How were you previous? What do you mean previous?'

Mum came and sat down next to me, putting a hand on my arm, 'It was a shotgun wedding, Love. We had to get permission from our parents because we were underage. You have to be twenty one otherwise.'

I let out a bark of laugher, 'You mean you did it before you were married.' I turned to Dad, 'You bastard. You bloody, bloody hypocrite. All the times you called me a slag or worse just because I was a minute or two late in, and you...'

He had the good grace to look away, 'I was just trying to protect you.'

I laughed again, 'You've never tried to protect me in your life, you two-faced git.' I turned to Mum, 'Would you have married him if you hadn't got in the family way?'

She cleared her throat, 'Well, I didn't, you know, know your Dad very well.' her blush returned.

I stood up, looking again from one to the other, 'Are you going to tell me I'm the result of a one-night-stand?'

The silence that followed was all the answer I needed.

'Did he rape you?' I asked, my voice hoarse.

'No, it wasn't like that, Lily. Honestly. Me and your Dad, we'd known each other a little bit and there was a bit of a spark. One night we went to the dance hall, had a bit to drink and then one thing led to another.'

'So if you'd kept your legs crossed you might have met someone else and had a decent husband. I might have had a decent father.'

She stood and turned off the kettle, 'That's very coarse. There's no need to be rude, Lily.'

Anger got the better of me. All the years I'd put up with insults and worse from this man, and Mum hardly ever standing up to him. Or standing up for me.

'I was just grateful he did the right thing Lily,' she twisted her wedding ring, 'lots of blokes didn't. I'd have been in a right pickle otherwise.'

'So you were grateful to end up with this... this... apology for a man!'

'Lily!' Dad said. 'Don't be rude to your mother. Or me, come to that.'

I turned on him, 'Don't you ever, EVER, tell me what to do. Never!'

'Let's all sit down and talk, shall we? I'll be gone before the week is out and we may never see each other again.' His voice was more reasonable than I'd ever heard it. Mum sat down but I stood, leaning against the sink, my arms crossed.

'So what? Think we'd even notice?'

He turned to look at Mum. 'I've put you down as next-of-kin in case something happens. I thought I should warn you.'

'Me? Why me? What about your fancy woman? Surely you'd put her down.' she sat back in the chair and folded her arms too.

'Well, it's like this, me and her went our separate ways.'

It was Mum's turn to laugh, 'So you thought you'd come back here, try to get your feet under the table.'

'It would be nice to think someone would care if I copped it.' his shoulder slumped and he bit his lip, 'someone to come home to, sort of thing.'

I unfolded my arms, 'Let's get this straight. You aren't getting your feet under the table. We don't care if you die, and you can forget coming back here. Get the message? We want nothing to do with you. Now bugger off!'

For a second the old him returned. His jaw tightened and his eyes narrowed. You could see the effort it cost him to keep calm. He turned to Mum, 'Surely you don't feel like that, do you, Love? We had a long time together.'

She picked up some potatoes and started to wash them in the sink, 'I feel exactly the same as Lily. You'd better go. Now.'

He sat for a moment, perhaps thinking we would change our mind. I handed him his hat, 'The front door's that way. Use it!' I went to open it and stood there. It took him a minute or two to see that we really meant it then he slowly stood up, put on his hat and walked past me without catching my eye. I slammed the door behind him, 'Good riddance to bad rubbish!' I muttered.

I went back in the kitchen. Mum was busy peeling the potatoes as if her life depended on it. It was clear the last thing she wanted to do was look at me.

'How come you've never told me all this?' I asked.

Her chin dropped, 'Well, it's a bit embarrassing, isn't it? And in the early days me and your Dad got on okay. Good enough anyway.'

She emptied the dirty potato water down the sink and put the potatoes in a saucepan, 'I don't know. Stress of living, finding money to pay the bills. He didn't want to get married any more than I did.'

'Didn't you think of seeing someone? Try to get rid of it?'

She shook her head, 'No, couldn't do that. And that 'it' is you, you daft thing. What a good thing I didn't get rid of you. You've been the best thing in my life.'

I went over and put my arm round her shoulder. I felt all the tension leave her body and felt bad for the way I spoke to her. 'I'm sorry Mum, I should have been more understanding.'

She turned round, 'It's okay, you'd just had a big shock. We should have told you years ago. It's not like ours was the first shotgun wedding ever. They're more common than you think. You know, I got hold of a copy of my mum and dad's marriage certificate and they'd only gone and altered the date so it looked like they'd been married a year longer than they had. My mum was four months gone when she married my dad. It's a pity this spoiled your last evening.'

Jean linked her arm through mine as we got off the bus, 'You sure you're okay with this? We don't have to go. No-one would think any the worse of you.'

I shook my head, 'I want to go. I want to say goodbye to him. There won't be another chance.'

It was overcast, the perfect weather for a funeral. Not that I'd been to many, but somehow I always noticed the weather. Too cold and I couldn't bear the thought of the loved one being put in the frozen ground, sunny and it seemed too cheerful for such a solemn occasion.

It was a pretty church in on the outskirts of London; an area that had escaped the bombing so far. With a grassy graveyard bordered by a stone wall, we could have been in the countryside. Daffodils waved in the breeze promising spring. Inside the church, weak sun shone through the windows scattering slowly moving coloured patterns on the old stone floor. The smell of the creamy beautiful lilies was almost overpowering. The church was about half full and I wondered who everyone was. People from David's work, friends and family I guessed. A couple of ARP people were the only ones I recognised.

The organist started playing *For the beauty of the earth* and we all stood. As the pallbearers bought the coffin in, I tried not to look at it. Tried not to think of lovely David there in that wooden box, soon to be in the earth for ever. I stifled my sobs in my hankie and constantly wiped away my tears. I hardly heard what the vicar said, or the elderly man who said a few words. I realised as he finished he must be David's father. I was vaguely aware of singing *Abide with me* but I couldn't remember the rest of the service.

As Jean and I walked towards the graveside, Jim joined us, 'Lily,' he said, 'so glad you could make it. How are you feeling now? How's your head?'

'I'm a lot stronger, thanks. My friend Jean here is a nurse so she's been making sure I behave myself. Jean, this is Jim, he's my ATS boss.'

Jim shook her hand and then patted my shoulder, 'You will come to the wake, won't you? Seeing as what happened to David, it's important us ARP people are represented.'

I went silent for a minute, then Jean said, 'It's okay Lil, we don't ‘ave to stay long. You can say a proper goodbye.'

'But I don't remember what happened. What if people ask me?'

'Just say you had a bang on the head and don't remember. No need to say more.'

Irrationally I dreading meeting his people. I felt transparent, as though everyone would know that David and I had been intimate. That they'd be judging me when he and I weren't married. I looked around at the other mourners, but of course none of them were looking at me.

As we continued to walk across the churchyard I noticed a middle aged man in a black suit look at me and smile. He didn't say anything but continued walking, catching up with a stony face woman with steel grey hair and a black felt hat with a feather in it.

The smell of freshly dug earth and the dreadful gaping hole in the ground waiting for David made me freeze a few feet away from the other mourners. I clenched my jaw, swallowing, on the verge of tears. After a couple of minutes I quietly slipped away and waited near the path. Jean came to join me, saying nothing, just being there holding my hand. The hum of the vicar's voice as David's coffin was lowered into the ground was shattered by a car backfiring nearby bringing us back to the moment.

Jim gave us a lift to the wake which was held in David's father's house, the house David grew up in. It was a spacious detached house with a generous garden front and back, very different to my family home. We went in last, feeling awkward as we were on the sidelines compared to David's family and people who had known him for years.

David's father met us at the door and shook our hands after asking us our names and how we knew David. But before we had time to say more, someone got his attention and he went into the living room. People were moving between that room, the hall and the dining room. Two women were busy laying out food, one cutting sandwiches into quarters, looking harassed and wiping her brow on her sleeve.

'Can I help?' I asked, wanting something to do to stop myself feeling so awkward.

She looked up and smiled, her frown disappearing, 'Oh, could you? It'd be such a help. I've still got to make a big pot of tea and start serving up.'

With no more introductions, she handed me the knife and I cut the sandwiches that were ready, then began buttering more bread. As I was working the man who'd smiled at me in the churchyard came over, 'I heard you are Lily. I'm so pleased to meet you. I'm Jonathan, David's brother.'

I wiped my hands on a tea towel then we shook hands, 'I'm so sorry,' I said, 'awful to lose your brother. You must miss him terribly.'

The lady who'd asked for help came back, 'You go and chat, Dear, it's all almost done.'

As Jonathan and I were speaking he led me away from the table into the kitchen. Jim and Jean followed and I noticed the stony faced woman in the feathered hat standing in the doorway.

I poured myself a glass of water and took a bite of a fish-paste sandwich.

'I wanted to speak to you,' Jonathan said, his eyes warm, 'I noticed that recently David had been happier than I've seen him since his wife had her accident. He told me he'd met you and you'd made him enjoy life again.'

I had no idea David had discussed me with anyone. 'How long is it since his wife died?' I asked.

He blinked rapidly, 'Died? She's not dead. Is that what he told you?'

I pushed my hair behind my ear, 'I must have misunderstood,' I said, a wobble in my voice, 'is his wife here?' I looked around the room.

The stony faced woman pushed Jim and Jean aside and stepped too close to me for comfort. 'No, she's not damn well here, is she? She's a vegetable. Brain damaged. The only thing in her life was David and you... you tart... you took him away...'

Jonathon put a hand on her arm, 'May, calm down, it's obvious Lily didn't know anything about this.'

She sneered, 'You expect me to believe that?' she turned back to me, 'Bet you were after his money, you look like you haven't got two halfpennies to rub together. How much did he spend on you? How much? Come on!'

Jonathon stepped between us, 'Lily, May is David's sister-in-law. Like all of us, she's grieving, otherwise she wouldn't...'

May put her hands on her hips, 'Wouldn't what? Say it like it is? This trollop needs to know we see right through her.'

She was so loud people had heard her from other rooms

and were listening to the conversation from the doorway. I wanted to run out of the door and rush back to Oxford.

Jim stepped forward, 'May, can I call you that? I've known David and Lily for some time and they were on duty together sometimes. They were both completely trustworthy. I'm so sorry that your brother-in-law died how he did. He was such a brave man, always wanting to help others. And some of the work he did for the ARP was dangerous. Very dangerous as you know.'

David's sister narrowed her eyes, 'So? He used to come to see my sister, his wife, every evening after work, but since he started this ARP business and HER!' she almost poked me in the chest, 'he's too busy! Too busy to see his own wife!'

I took a step back, 'But I... I didn't...'

'Didn't what? Care about my sister, lying there year after year. You... you... harlot!'

Jim took a glass of sherry from a sideboard, then he gently held her arm, 'May, this is very upsetting for you. Why don't we go and get some fresh air in the garden. Here, here's a drink for you.' She initially shook his arm off, but slowly let him lead her outside. Other people who were pretending they weren't listening drifted back inside the rest of the house now the show was over.

I was relieved to see her go but my knees shook and I had to sit down on one of the kitchen chairs, my face so red I wanted to get some cold air on it.

'Did you know about his wife?' Jean asked, her voice kind.

I shook my head, 'I'm sure he told me he was a widower.' I paused, 'But maybe he didn't actually say that. I think he said she was gone. I probably jumped to conclusions.'

'Jim is looking after May.' Jonathan said, 'Here, let me put the kettle on again and we can talk about this.'

My heart was still pounding so strongly it made me cough. 'Jonathan, I truly didn't know. I thought David was a widower.'

He got out some more cups, then came and sat opposite me, 'He was, effectively. Since her accident, his wife has shown no sign of any brain activity apart from still breathing. She didn't recognise anyone, speak or do anything.'

'But surely he didn't consider her dead.' I couldn't keep the strain out of my voice.

He got up again, found a small teapot in the cupboard and spooned tea leaves into it. 'The truth is, David was a saint. He was at her bedside every minute he wasn't at work. The strain was terrible. His job was stressful and seeing her so ill made him feel helpless. It was me who suggested he find somewhere to live nearer work and just come to see her two or three times a week. I was pleased when he told me he'd found something else to do in the evenings so he met other people. I never imaged he'd choose something as dangerous as ARP work though, but it was just like him to want to help others.'

I went back to work next day even though my arm was still in plaster. Journeys took for ever because buses had to navigate round more bomb damaged roads every day. Once I even saw a bus that had half fallen in a bomb crater and was thrown against a building. It looked as if it was trying to climb out of the hole and drive up the wall. I couldn't help but imagine all the passengers who must have been thrown to the back of the bus, piling on top of each other. I wondered how many were killed or injured. If it had happened in the evening the ARP wardens would have had their hands full.

The lady sitting next to me on the bus was busy darning a sock. Her stitches were so expert you could hardly tell the darn from the original. She smiled and indicated my plastered arm, 'You've been in the wars from the look of it. What happened to you then?'

No matter how many times I repeated the story, it still tore at my heart. 'Nothing drastic, I just fell over some debris.' I said. No need to tell a stranger my story.

'That's tough luck,' she said, biting the end of the wool between her teeth, and putting her work in her bag, 'don't know how we all carry on. I've been bombed out twice and my kids have been evacuated. I miss them something rotten.' she stopped and looked out of the window, 'Well, this is my stop. Take care, Love.'

Every time the bombing affected our bit of the city, the buses would have to find a different route to get to their destination if the road was up. Journeys got longer and longer and the view outside the bus window more and more depressing. There were queues everywhere. Women queued from early morning for food, despite sleepless nights down the shelter. Then they faced a day's work on top.

I caught sight of my reflection in the bus window and saw how haggard I looked. Sleep eluded me and I spent the night trying to unravel what I'd learned about David's wife. Did I misunderstand what he'd said, or had he deliberately misled me? More to the point, if he had told me the truth would it have made any difference to our time together? The questions went round and round in my head as I tried to sleep in the air raid shelter, then back in my own bed. Guilt weighed on me heavily. Not that his wife would ever have known. From what Jonathon said, she was never going to know anything ever again, poor woman.

The depot was boring but it was better than sitting at

Mum's place all day with nothing to do. Edith and Marian greeted me with a smile and wanted to know all about my injuries. They also insisted on writing on the plaster on my arm and I was glad to see their messages weren't rude. I'd seen so many plastered limbs with messages and pictures so rude on them they were enough to make you blush.

I was glad I hadn't told them about David, although I'd been tempted to many times. Ten minutes talking passed, then I looked at the clock and noticed that Mrs Rogan wasn't at her desk. Not only that, the other two were more relaxed than usual. Edith saw my glance, 'She's off sick,' she said, with a smile, 'shouldn't be happy when anyone's ill, but it's wonderful not having her miserable face around. Been gone a week, she has.'

'When's she coming back?' I hoped it wouldn't be soon.

Edith shrugged, 'We don't know. Haven't even been told what's wrong with her. I think it might be the... you know... the big C.'

Mrs Rogan might be a miserable woman but I couldn't wish that on her. 'Let's hope not. Any more news of your husband?' I asked.

Edith's smile was all the answer I needed. 'He managed to phone here one day! We could only speak for a couple of minutes and I couldn't hear him very well. But he's alive and that's all that counts.'

I was so pleased for her. Good news was hard to find with all the bombing. 'Will he be able to phone again, do you think?'

She pulled a face, 'Who knows? But I'm sure he's try whenever he can. This damned war has to be over one day.'

'I've got some news too!' Marian said, 'my brother's home on leave. It's so good to see him. Well, we try to. Trouble is, as soon as the police saw him in uniform they pounced on him and they've got him clearing up bombed houses all day long. He's a carpenter so they've got him putting front doors back on and that sort of thing too. He says it's easier being in the war! Talking of that, any news of your Edward?'

I was about to answer when the boss, walked in. He beamed a welcome. 'Lily! I'm so glad you're back, but you're not going to be able to type with that broken arm, are you?'

'Well, I could use one hand, I suppose.'

'That won't do. How will you put paper in and all the other things that need two hands? No, I've got something else I'd like you to do. Come with me to my office.'

'Sit down, sit down,' he said, sitting behind his desk and resting his hands on his round stomach. 'We're very glad to have you back and I want to ask you a favour. Would you be willing to take on some of Mrs Rogan's work?'

I frowned, 'But she's never shown me what she does, in fact she's a bit, well, secretive about it.'

He smiled, 'That's true, and in fact she was very keen for me to take her paperwork for her to do at home. But I wouldn't hear of it. Apart from not helping her health, we can't have official papers leaving the office like that. Anyway, not to worry, I can teach you what to do. It doesn't require much typing, mostly writing in financial journals, keeping records up to date and that sort of thing. What do you think?'

It sounded a lot less boring than typing all day, so I quickly agreed. 'Well,' he said as his phone rang, 'go and walk round the depot and let everyone know you're back. Meet me here in an hour and we'll make a start.'

It had started drizzling while I'd been inside so I fetched my coat and umbrella. My plastered arm wouldn't go through my sleeve and it hung loose like a horrible parody of the men who had lost limbs in the last war and now this one. I didn't expect sympathy from the men in the depot, that wasn't their style. But several came up and cracked jokes about my broken arm and one, Frank, insisted I join him and his mates for a cup of tea.

Their little hut was a bit grubby. I'm no housewife, but I itched to wash down the paintwork which was decorated with a multitude of greasy fingerprints. Two calendars with pictures of near naked women were on one wall and loads of pin-up pictures cut out from newspapers were everywhere. Frank saw me looking, 'Sorry about this, Sweetheart. Blokes will be blokes, you know what it's like.'

'Got any urgent orders today?' one of them asked him.

'Yeah, three. Just in. I've written them on the board over there. They can wait til we've had our break though.'

I'd never really understood how the depot worked beyond goods in and goods out. It had never been part of my job. 'I didn't know you had urgent orders,' I said, 'does that happen often?'

Frank offered me a broken biscuit, 'Been to Woolworth's, I see.' I said with a smile, taking a Rich Tea.

He nodded, 'I was in luck, they had in some yesterday. You wanted to know about urgent orders. We get them every day. Three so far today, but more will come in during the day.'

I dunked my biscuit in my tea, managing not to drop the lot in. 'How do you manage that then? Does one person have responsibility for urgent orders or what?'

'Got another biscuit?' someone interrupted.

'Get your own!' Frank called back, 'one a day's your lot or the missus will have my guts for garters.' He turned back to me. 'I supervise this lot see, and some others who have second shift for their break. I decide who'll do the urgent stuff. Depends on what else they're doing when the order comes in.'

I didn't like to ask any more questions, but sat wondering if this could be anything to do with stuff going missing. I realised that sitting have a cuppa like this would help me learn more than I'd learned in all the times I'd walked around the warehouses.

Mr McDonald was ready for me when I got back, papers spread across his desk.

'Sit yourself down. We'll just do the basics now so you can make a bit of a start, then later today I'll show you a bit more. I always find the best way to remember something is to do it. Do you want to make notes?'

Luckily it was my left arm that was broken and I'm right handed. The paper I tried to write on kept shifting about as I wrote and eventually he pinned it down for me with his ash tray. The disgusting acid smell made my nose wrinkle, but I didn't think I could say anything.

'Right,' he said, 'you know we get loads of goods in every day. The boxes all have an order number on them. Well, they should have, but sometimes they get ripped off or they're unreadable. In that case you'll be notified. Then you'll have to try to match the boxes in the warehouse with the order sheet.'

'So that's why Mrs Rogan regularly left her desk.' I said.

'That's right. It can be a lengthy job. The blokes'll tell you if there's an unmarked box. You might be able to match them without going to the warehouses. Trouble is, sometimes the blokes don't give a good enough description. Or what they call it isn't the same as what you've got written down.'

'Do they always know what's in the boxes?'

He nodded, 'Yes, it's printed on the side. The boxes should be unopened, but...'

'You think some of them may have been opened and resealed. Some taken out.'

'You've got it! But you're looking tired. Why don't you go and have your break, then this afternoon you can work on what we've covered. Tomorrow, we'll go into more detail.'

I went back in to see Edith and Marian. They were both hammering the keys on their typewriters so hard their whole machines bounced up and down. They looked up when I walked in.

'So what did he want you to do?' Marian asked.

'Take over Mrs Rogan's work.'

Her jaw dropped open, 'Blimey, she won't like that a bit. She'll make your life a misery when she gets back. You got to sit in her seat, too?'

Edith pulled the letter she'd been typing out of her typewriter and peeled the sheets from the carbon paper. 'She's right, you know. Mrs R's always been so secretive about what she does. You'd never know we all worked in the same place. Takes this Careless Talk Costs Lives too far if you ask me.'

Grinning, I went and sat in Mrs Rogan's seat and tried to make myself look important. It didn't work; they just laughed at me. I gave up and went back to my desk. 'If she picks on me, I'll have to tell Mr McDonald, after all, he's telling me to do it. Will you two back me up?'

'Of course we will,' Edith said, 'she'll have to pick on us all then, won't she! It'll be three against one.'

I was surprised to see Bronwyn in when I got home that evening. Even more surprised to find her sniffling into a hankie, with red eyes and a generally hang-dog look. She was already in her night things, her dressing gown wrapped tightly round her. I dumped my stuff and sat beside her.

'What's wrong? You look awful.'

She attempted to smile. 'Thanks for that, Lil. Makes me feel so much better. Got a cold.' She blew her nose, but I wasn't convinced.

'Come on, out with it. What's going on? Did you fall off your bike or something?'

I got the story out of her bit by bit. Donald, the married man she'd been seeing, dumped her and went back to his wife.

'I thought you said he'd left her already.'

She wiped her nose, 'That's what he told me and he said he could always see me when he was in London. Told me his home was in Warrington and he had to keep living there to be near his kids.'

I blinked hard, 'What, you mean he didn't live there?'

'No, it's like this see, he only lives in Essex, doesn't he. I never thought he'd stay in London overnight if he'd lived so near so why wouldn't I believe him.'

I was having trouble keeping up with this. 'Blimey, even with the mess the trains are in surely he could have got home at night. Was his boss happy to pay his hotel bills if he could have gone home?'

She wrapped her dressing gown more tightly round herself, 'That was another lie. He didn't even have a boss, it was his own business. And he just told his wife he had to go away to another part of the country for work when he came to see me.'

'And she believed him, poor woman. But how did you find out what he was up to?'

'He let slip one night and called me her name. That could happen I suppose but it made me suspicious. So I went through his pockets when he was asleep after we'd, you know, and I found a letter in one of his pockets. To an address in Essex. He tried to bluff when I challenged him but he had liar written all over his face, the bastard. Owned up in the end he was still married and living with his wife. I'll never trust another man as long as I live.'

My heart sank, she was in so much pain, 'Poor you, that's awful. But Bron, I didn't think you really cared about any of these men. You never let on.'

She sobbed again, 'I didn't care before. But Don was different. Kind, reliable, fun to be with. I thought I'd found the right bloke for me and I didn't think that'd happen. It goes to show how wrong you can be.'

'But you've never said a word about getting serious with him.' I said, amazed at her change of attitude.

'I'm going to say something serious now. Some things are hard to talk about. And you've never approved of me going out with married men.'

'I...'

She interrupted me. 'Don't protest, I know you didn't like it. Anyway, you had enough to worry about what with Edward missing and David dying. It seemed easier to keep it to myself like.'

She reached into her dressing gown pocket and pulled out a bracelet. 'Only gave me this as a goodbye present, didn't he. Made me feel like a bought woman.'

I remembered all the times she'd said she only went out with married men because of the things they gave her, but thought better than to remind her of that. I took the bracelet off her. 'This is a lovely piece of jewellery. Gold. I'll bet it's worth a bit.'

She knocked it aside, 'It'll always be a "clear off" bracelet to me. I'll never like it.'

I put my hand on hers. 'Don't be like that, Love. Put it away for a few weeks and see how you feel then. If you still hate it, you can sell it and buy something you like. But I'll bet a penny to a pound by then you'll feel a bit better and just start remembering the good times.'

She sniffed, wiped her nose and got up. She went to the sink and splashed cold water on her face. 'Tell you what, let's go out and get blind drunk.'

Just then the air raid sirens started. We looked at each other, 'Sod it, Lil.' Bronwyn said, heading towards the bedroom, 'If tonight's the night we buy it, so be it. Get your glad rags on, we're going out. Let's go and dance the night away. Your arm is out of plaster so you'll be tickety boo.'

Fifteen minutes later we were out in the street wearing our best stuff, gas masks on our hips and shielded torches helping us find the way. There were no bombs near us, but we could see the familiar red glow in the sky to the east. Then, all of a sudden it was as if the air changed and a barrage balloon got hit. It burst into flames and drifted to earth like some grotesque dancer, twisting slowly this way and that. I sent up a little prayer that it didn't fall on anyone.

We managed to get a bus and went to a dance hall. I never did know the name of it, but Bronwyn had been there with one of her blokes. A lot of people were in uniform because they got in free, but plenty were in civvies. There were a scattering of sofas against the walls and a few tiny round tables with chairs, all occupied. Spotlights wove coloured lights across the dancers, picking up the bright dresses and shining military badges. On the stage the band leader was waving his baton and singing, although the band overwhelmed his voice. The sound of so many dancing feet was in competition with both.

The all-clear sounded but no-one had taken any notice of

the siren in the first place. Bronwyn and I splashed out and had a gin and tonic each, then a second one. Soon a couple of lads offered to buy us another and before you could say Bob's-your-uncle we were on the dance floor being thrown around and loving it. Every minute my mood lifted and I could see from Bronwyn's smile that she felt the same. This was just what we needed. Life in the Blitz was depressing and scary, but it made you appreciate being alive if only because you might not be the next day.

At the end of the evening our dancing partners wanted to come back with us, but we refused. We both had work next morning and I certainly didn't want to have to spend time fighting mine off.

As Bronwyn and I got into bed, ready for a few hours sleep, Bronwyn said, 'I've got some leave due. Can you get a few days off? We could go away somewhere peaceful where we could sleep through the night.'

Only a week later we achieved our dream; a few days away from the constant fear of being bombed. We found a farm where there were a few chalets usually used for fruit pickers during the summer. It was too early for fruit to be ripe so the farmer let the chalets out at a reasonable price. The chalets weren't much more than glorified sheds but we were delighted. The weather was glorious, despite it only being towards the end of April. Sunny days and cold nights. With every hour I could feel the tension of all I'd been through slipping away.

Being there reminded me of a couple of holidays we'd had when I was a kid. Hop picking in Kent. I remember being excited when we set off for the train and a change from our everyday life. We stayed in Hopper Huts, even more basic than the chalets Bronwyn and I were in. But old people told us they were a big improvement on what they'd had before. Picking was hard work, especially when it rained or the sun was too hot for comfort. But mum made sure we had big hats and always wore something to cover our shoulders to avoid sunburn. One corner of the field was always set up as the nursery with some women looking after the little ones. Their cots were just sacking hanging from criss-cross branches. Other women prepared the meal for when the working day was done. Mum loved not having to think what to cook each day. Then when us kids were supposed to be asleep we'd listen to them all laughing over bottles of beer until we nodded off, muscles aching from the unfamiliar work. But when mum and dad came back to our hut, he'd be ready to start a drunken fight, often hitting mum and calling her names. Next day, no-one ever mentioned it even though they must have heard.

Thank goodness those days were gone and mum didn't have to put up with him and his bad temper any longer.

~

On our first full day Bronwyn and I made sandwiches and set out for a picnic. It was warm enough to keep our jackets in our bags, and the feel of the sun on our skin was a reminder that winter was retreating. It rained during the night and the air was full of damp, earthy smells. Pink Blossom in the trees gave off a soft, sweet musky odour that was a real tonic after London smells of traffic and burning. The verges were covered in chalky yellow Celandine and the birds sang sweetly. We spotted a bluebell wood and found a clearing where the sun reached. It was the perfect place for a picnic. We ate our cheese sandwiches and drank our water surrounded by a sea of blue flowers gently waving in the breeze.

'You got any idea what you'll do when this war is over?' Bronwyn asked, her mouth half full.

It seemed I thought of little else, yet I couldn't give a good answer. So much depended on if Britain won. If the Jerries won, we'd be under Nazi rule and I couldn't imagine what that would be like. I didn't want to imagine it either. If we won, it was going to take ages to get the country sorted out because so much damage had been done.

'I don't know,' I said, 'but I suppose us girls will have a lot more choice of jobs now. Look at all the things we've been doing that before the war people thought only men could do. I'm not going back to sewing buttons or sleeves on men's shirts, that's for sure!'

'I'd forgotten you did that,' she said, 'I did all sorts; worked in a pub, a shop, a factory, anything to get a bit of money and stop my mum moaning at me. Anyway, if I'd been at home all day I'd have had to look after my little brothers and sisters, little buggers that they are. Tell you the truth, I think I might try to stay in the army, see if I can get trained to do something useful.'

The sun went behind a cloud and we picked up our stuff and walked towards the nearest village, our feet crunching on the gravel pathway. We passed the village church with its weathered gravestones hugged by grasses, a few with vases of daffodils showing their family still remembered them. As we walked past I ran my hand on along the stone wall, smooth yet bumpy under my fingertips. I wondered how many thousands of people must have done the same over the years and what their stories were.

We were just commenting on a sign advertising a fete in

the village hall when we heard a motorbike brake near us. Two airmen stopped to let a bent old lady cross the street. She got half way, wobbled and then fell over. She cried out in pain as she landed on one knee and her shopping scattered around her. We began to hurry towards her but the two airmen on the motorbike got there first. Propping up their bike they helped her up, talking kindly to her the whole time. Then they picked up her shopping and helped her back onto the pavement, winked at me and Bronwyn then went on their way.

'Are you okay?' we asked when we caught up with her. 'Do you want us to walk you home or anything?'

She was dressed all in brown with a white lacy collar on her dress and a knitted tea-cosy type hat. Her deep smile lines and twinkly eyes made me wish she was my grandmother. She gave us a lovely smile, 'I'm fine dears, I was just going to the village hall. There's a bit of a fete there. I can get a cuppa and a sit down. Might find something good at the bring-and-buy table too. Are you coming?'

The village hall was decorated with colourful bunting and lots of Union Jacks. A few games were on the green - throw-the-wellie-into a ring, get a ball in a bucket, and hoopla were all well attended by giggling children.

A few small tables and chairs were outside on the grass, a sure sign that spring was really here. Each table had a little posy of wild flowers in a jam jar. We helped the lady to a chair and went inside to get her tea. The hall was busy, full of village people who knew each other and were taking the chance to catch up with news. There was a toss-a-ring table, the bring-and-buy table, guess the weight of the cake, a plant stall, Tombola, second hand books, lucky dip, raffle sales, a fortune teller and of course the tea and cake stall.

As we queued to get our drinks Bronwyn turned to me,

'Not being funny nor nothing, but them flyboys were a bit of alright, weren't they!'

A middle aged lady near us turned and I expected her to give us a frown but she grinned. 'I remember what we got up to in the last war, my dears. Enjoy life while you can.'

We took the old lady her tea and a biscuit then went back inside. I was browsing through the books when a voice said, 'Pick a card, any card.' I turned and there was the oldest magician I'd ever seen. His dress coat bulged over his tummy and his top hat fell low enough to rest on his ears. But his eyes sparkled with enjoyment. He held the fanned cards out again, 'Come on, my dears, any card you like.'

A cluster of small children gathered to watch so I made a great play of choosing my card. I showed it to them with many warnings not to say out loud what it was. After much confusion, he named my card accurately. I could never understand how they did that. Then he turned to a girl standing there. He juggled with two balls, one blue and one red. He handed them to her telling her to check they were normal balls, then he put down the blue ball and cupped the red one in his hand. He did a few dramatic sweeps with this hands and said a few nonsense incantations.

'Okay, Sweetheart, which hand has the red ball?' he asked the girl. She confidently tapped his left hand. He opened it, and it was empty. Not so sure of herself, she tapped the other hand. Her eyes bulged when she saw that was empty too. She urged the other children to look on the floor in case he's dropped it and even looked at his back.

'It's up his sleeve,' one lad said, full of bravado, 'go on, Mister, shake your arms. I bet it'll fall out.'

The elderly magician smiled and obliged. No ball fell out. 'How d'you do that then?' the boy asked.

'I can't tell you that, young fellow-me-lad, it's a state

secret and we all know careless talk costs lives!'

He doffed his top hat at me and Bronwyn and went on to entertain another group.

'I know that ball trick,' Bronwyn said, picking up a ghastly ornament from the bring-and-buy table, 'used to go out with a magician.'

She put the ornament down and brushed her hands against her skirt. 'That ornament is gomping, no wonder they gave it away.'

We reached the Tombola, and I had five goes and won a bar of soap. With soap so hard to come by I was delighted. 'Go on then, tell me how the magician did it.'

'It's all to do with what they call misdirection. They get your attention somewhere while they do something you won't notice. Like do a big flourish or something with one hand while they're hiding something with the other.'

'Is that what he did then?'

She picked her Tombola numbers out of a bucket and swore quietly when she realised she hadn't won anything. 'Tidy darts you won that soap, hope you're going to share it,' she said, 'Yes, he was asking the girl about which ball was where but he'd already put it in his pocket when she was looking somewhere else. So of course it wasn't in either hand. If that lad had asked him to turn out his pockets he'd have had to make an excuse quick.'

'So the trick was to get someone to believe something was somewhere when it wasn't there at all.'

She laughed, 'Yeah, I used to pull the wool over my mum's eyes something rotten getting her to believe I was somewhere when all the time I was out with a lad.'

We went round all the stalls. I bought an Agatha Christie book at the second hand stall, and Bronwyn bought a pot of strawberry jam. We sat in the sun with another cup of tea, talking about the way Agatha Christie misdirected her readers just as surely as the magician we'd just seen. Then we slowly walked back to our chalets, enjoying the peace of the countryside.

'You've never know what was going on in London and Coventry living here, wouldn't you?' I said.

'Lucky for them, I reckon.'

As we walked towards our chalet we were surprised to find the airmen who'd helped the old lady across the road had moved into the next one. They'd taken some chairs from inside and were sitting in the dying sun, chatting and smoking. As soon as they saw us they sprang up, 'Good afternoon, ladies,' the dark haired one said, 'can we offer you a drink?'

Two minutes later we'd got our chairs and were sharing their beer. The dark-haired one was Richard and the blond one was Albert. Somehow I ended up chatting to Richard and saw that Bronwyn and Albert were getting on well too.

'Fancy coming to the pub later?' Richard asked. Me and Bronwyn looked at each other and nodded. 'See you in an hour.'

'Great,' he said, 'we can walk there together.'

We went back to our chalet and I put on my last pair of nylons. 'Expecting anything special tonight?' Bronwyn asked with a grin.

The pub was busy, but we managed to find space in the corner squashed between a table with four old men wearing flat caps and another with four old women wearing felt hats. Maybe they were actually four couples who had split up for the evening to chat to their mates.

The evening was cool and we were glad to be fairly near the fireplace, despite the way the coal was splitting burning specks. From the state of the rag rug in front of it, this wasn't anything new.

Albert stood up, 'I'll get the first round, what'll you all have?'

We gave our orders and he and Bronwyn went to the bar leaving me with Richard. I soon found out he was a pilot and Albert was his gunner. 'That's dangerous work,' I said, 'you must be very brave.'

He laughed, 'Crazy, you mean. Someone worked out our life expectancy is four weeks, but we all fly assuming we're the ones who will make it back. What about your work?'

I told him all about the depot and the ARP work, 'That ARP work is dangerous too,' he said, 'your life must be in danger every time you're out there.' My heart tightened as I thought of David dying beside me, but couldn't bring myself to talk about it and changed the subject.

Albert and Bronwyn came back with our drinks and we played dominos as we talked. Maybe it was the cider but I was soon very relaxed with Richard, and it felt as if I'd known him for years. We played darts and they all laughed at me every time my dart missed the board, which was quite often. Often enough for people sitting nearby to edge their chairs away to my embarrassment. When the landlord called 'Time gentlemen, please.' we headed back to our chalets. The temperature had dropped more and Richard gave me his scarf with a smiling flourish. We were walking down a dark part of the lane to the chalets when thunder rumbled a long way off and a flash of lightening terrified me. It was like I was experiencing that last bomb all over again. I cried out, stumbled and almost fell. Richard grabbed my arm just in time, saving me from taking a tumble. After double checking I wasn't hurt, he put his arm round my shoulder, sharing his warmth, 'I'll keep you safe.' he said and I could hear the smile in his voice. But it took several minutes for my inner trembling to calm down.

I was grateful the storm didn't come any nearer, not

wanting the old terror to spoil what was left of the evening. As we walked I could hear the gurgle of a stream to our left and the gentle sound of the breeze in the trees that were bursting with new life.

It was the most natural thing in the world for Richard to come into my chalet and Bronwyn and Albert to go into theirs.

Richard and I stood at the window and he wrapped his arms round me as we looked out at the night. The moon hung lightly in the sky, its image vanishing and reappearing as the wind brushed branches from the tree across our vision. An owl hooted and a fox yapped close by, unfamiliar sounds to a city dweller light me. I jumped when a bat flew close to the window and Richard laughed and held me tighter. I could smell his leather coat, the beer he'd drunk and, as I turned to kiss his cheek, the unique smell of his skin. In the moonlight I couldn't see the dimple in his chin or the warmth in his eyes, but I could feel his need and it matched my own. He brushed my ear as he spoke, 'Lily,' he said, his tone serious for a minute, 'I have to leave early tomorrow morning and we may never see each other again. Are you sure this is what you want to do?'

I was sure. My answer was to kiss his soft lips, his moustache tickling my nose.

I'd like to be able to blame the alcohol for what happened. Or blame the feeling that Richard might die next day when he was due to fly again. Or blame grieving for David. But none of that would be true. It just seemed the most natural thing in the world for us to get undressed in that chilly chalet and jump under the covers of my tiny bed, teeth chattering. His body was warm after the chilly air and we clung together giggling as we pulled the covers over our heads to keep the cold out.

When I woke up next morning he was gone. On my pillow he'd left a little posy of wild flowers he must have picked in the pre-dawn. I smiled as I remembered our love-making, urgent at first then slow and sensuous. As I moved, the scent of our union drifted to my nose, making me smile and stretch languidly. I lay there wondering how it was I didn't feel guilty. I kept prodding at corners of my mind, like someone with toothache can't resist poking their tongue in the affected one. But no, there was no guilt. My values were changing, I realised. I'd been bought up to think sex before marriage was a sin. But as long as it doesn't hurt anyone else, what was the harm in it? I couldn't think of any.

I swung my legs down and got out of bed, wrapping a blanket round myself as a make-shift dressing gown. The orange cotton curtains gave the bare room a warm glow despite the early morning chill. I opened them and stood at the window Richard and I looked out of the night before. Now early morning mist softened the scene and the sun was just beginning to peak through here and there, sending gentle shafts of light through the trees. Birds singing gave a welcome early morning change to the all-clear I was used to in London.

As I stood looking out and remembering my night with Richard I remembered that Edward and I had never got as far as making love. Although only months before, we both still held the pre-war attitudes that we should wait until we were married. So we waited, fighting our temptation, and now he was missing, presumed dead. I couldn't help but regret that wait. Our love-making would have made us both so happy and if he was dead, it would have been a joyful memory for him to take with him. I sighed and turned to get dressed just as Bronwyn walked into the chalet, a knowing grin on her face.

Bronwyn teased me about my 'easy virtue' as she called it all the way back to London and I couldn't really come back with a good argument. Although we didn't see Richard or Albert again our few days away reinvigorated us and we felt ready to face the chaos that was our everyday life. But our happy state didn't last long. We opened the door to our rooms and there was Bronwyn's brother Alun lounging on the settee like he owned the place. You could hardly see across the room for cigarette smoke. Dirty dishes piled up in the sink and the stink of his unwashed feet made my nose wrinkle.

I dropped my case with a bang. 'What're you doing here?' I asked, my voice icy.

He took the fag out of his mouth, 'Staying a few days, ain't I?' he looked at Bronwyn, 'you don't mind, do you, Sis?'

She walked over and knocked his feet off the arm of the settee, 'Girlfriend finally have the sense to throw you out, did she?'

For an answer he reached to a bag beside him and took out some nylons and tins of corned beef. 'These are for you girls. Know you'd like them.'

'Why are you here?' Bronwyn asked, ignoring his gifts.

He grinned, 'Caught me out, didn't she. Threw all my stuff out on the landing when I was out without so much as a minute's warning. Wouldn't answer the door nor nothing. Bitch.'

I glared at him, but if he noticed he didn't give a damn. 'I want you out.' I said.

Ignoring me, he looked at Bronwyn, 'Just two more nights, Sis. Got rooms sorted out after that. Honest.'

She snorted, 'The day you're honest is the day I'll die of

shock. You can stay here two more nights as long as we get two more pairs of stockings each and whatever else you've got in that bag.'

She didn't dare look at me as she spoke. 'But...' I started.

Alun waved his arm in agreement, scattering fag ash on the floor. 'It's a deal.' he reached into his bag and pulled out some tins of beans and more corned beef. He held them out towards me with a wink. His charm may have worked with some girls, but not me. 'If you're not out of here within forty eight hours we'll thrown your things onto the landing too. I don't care if Bronwyn is your sister, this is my place too.'

My words may have been righteous, but I was hypocritical enough to take the food and stockings again. Going into my bedroom I put the stockings in the jam jar where I always kept them so they wouldn't ladder. Then I sat on the bed remembering the night with Richard, a small smile curling the corners of my mouth.

As I began unpacking there was a loud hammering on the door. I did a mental check; no, it wasn't rent day and we hadn't invited anyone round. I walked through from the bedroom and saw Bronwyn wasn't in the living room. She'd probably gone to the bathroom and forgotten her key.

So I was more than surprised to see two burly police officers standing there, their faces serious. Apart from their very smart uniforms they could have been Laurel and Hardy. The tall one had piercing blue eyes that wouldn't miss a thing. The little round one had crumbs down his front and a scattering of dandruff on his shoulders.

'We're here to see Alun Jones,' the taller of the two said. He'd barely finished the sentence when a sound behind me made me turn round. To my amazement, Alun's legs were disappearing through the window, smelly socks complete with holes in the heels in mid air. The officer saw what was happening, pushed me aside, and ran towards the window, truncheon in hand. He whacked Alun's insoles with the truncheon resulting in a scream from the other wide of the window. Then he grabbed Alun and pulled him back inside, swearing and cursing. They shoved him onto one of our kitchen chairs, the shorter one holding him down by the shoulder. Alun rubbed the soles of his feet, agony etched on his brow, but that didn't stop the torrent of abuse coming out of his filthy mouth. He wriggled and tried to escape, and the officer grabbed one arm and twisted it behind his back.

Bronwyn came back from the bathroom and stood in the doorway with her mouth open. 'What the hell's happening here?' she asked, her hands on her hips.

'Who might you be?' asked the tall policeman.

She pointed at Alun, 'I'm his sister. What's going on here?'

The policeman ignored her question and turned back to Alun.

'Now just you behave, laddie,' he said, 'we have reason to believe that you have given false information about the state of your health when you were called up,'

Alun sat silent for once, his face contorted from pain from his feet, his mouth opening and closing without a word. But his eyes were searching for a means of escape. He looked at me and Bronwyn, pleading in his eyes. I just leaned against the doorframe, arms folded, expressionless. He was not only a draft dodger but also a looter and, if my suspicion was correct, he stole from the newly dead. Maybe even helped them on their way to meet their maker. He was lucky if this was all the police wanted him for. His other offences were much more serious, he'd face hanging if he were convicted.

Finally he found his voice, 'I'm not Alun Jones, I'm...' he started. The policeman curled his top lip, 'And I'm Arthur Askey,' he said, 'we know who you are and we know what you did. That bloke with the bad chest who did the medical for you has been singing like a canary.'

'But I never...' Alun tried.

They stood either side of him and pulled him up, none too gently. 'You're coming with us now,' the tall one said, 'time to get this sorted out once and for all. You'll soon be joining the other men at the front, you cowardly little lump of shit. Hands out in front of you.'

The handcuffs were on in no time and the policemen gripped Alun so tight as they marched him out the door, his feet barely touched the floor. He looked over his shoulder, 'Help me, Bron.' he shouted.

It was all over so quickly it was hard to take in. I looked at Bronwyn to see if she was upset, but to my surprise she started laughing.

'Don't mean to be funny, nor nothing, but he's had that coming for a long while. Good job they didn't search the place or we'd have lost our stockings.'

'But aren't you worried about him?' I asked.

She shook her head, 'No, he'll probably wriggle out of it somehow. But if he doesn't, the army'll do him good. If anyone needed the discipline, it's him. He should think himself lucky the Bobbies weren't after him for his thieving.'

The door was still open and Alun's ex-girlfriend from across the hall came in, 'Got him, did they?' she asked, 'Couldn't help but hear the noise them Bobbies made.'

Bronwyn looked at her, 'Did they knock on your door first then?'

'Yes, they had my address, but I soon told them he was with you, the little rotter. Good riddance, I reckon. Sorry when he's your brother and all, but he's a bad 'un. Two-timed me more than once.' And with that, she turned on her heels and went back into her room.

'So each time a consignment arrives, the men in the yard check it against the docket and pass the paperwork to Mrs Rogan. Well, to you while she's off sick.'

After the short break away with Bronwyn, it was back to learning how to do Mrs Rogan's job. It didn't seem very complicated although I could see I'd need to give a lot of attention to detail. Never the thing I'm best at.

I looked at the paper Mr McDonald was showing me, 'What happens if the consignment is short?' I asked.

'Then the guys mark that on the docket,' he riffled through the pile of dockets in front of him until he found what he wanted, 'here, like this one. See, it's one box short.'

'Do I have to chase the missing stuff? What do I do? Phone the supplier?'

He shook his head, 'We only do that if it's very urgent because we like a paper trail. Write and tell them what's missing. Most suppliers are good and will send the stuff immediately. Then you'll get another docket,' again, he riffled through the papers, pulling one out, 'see, like this one, it shows it's to replace what's missing. Then when the goods are sent out to the army unit that requests them, you tie the two together and if everything matches you can sign them off and file the papers.'

I headed back to the office trying to remember all I'd learned. Edith and Marian looked up when I walked in, 'How'd you get on?' Edith asked, 'Has he made you our supervisor?'

I laughed, 'Of course not, you two know loads more than me.'

'Who's going to dish out work then?' Marian asked.

I shrugged, 'No idea, I expect he'll tell us. Anyway, we can work it out ourselves, can't we? We always said that.'

A ray of sun broke through the clouds, spreading cheer on Edith's desk. She looked out the window, 'Perhaps it's going to be a nice day after all. You got to go round the warehouses this morning? You won't need your umbrella.'

'I'll do some paperwork first. Don't talk to me girls, 'cos I'll be sure to make a mistake if you do!'

I spent an hour checking dockets coming in like I'd been taught. Best to practice what I learned before I forgot it. Then I went round the warehouse collecting new dockets in so far. Some of the men handed them over quite happily, glad to stop work and have a chat but others were harder to convince. 'What happened to Mrs Rogan? Who said you can collect these?' were some of the comments I heard. When I went back to the office I told Edith and Marion.

'What's it to them?' Edith asked, 'anyone'd think they were on the fiddle. Makes no difference to them who has the paperwork.'

She looked at the clock. 'Come on girls, time for our dinner break. I'm taking my sandwiches to the park while the sun's shining. You coming?'

The sun had been playing hide-and-seek all the time I'd been in the yard, but now the clouds cleared away, vanished like a ghost in the sunshine. For the first time of the year we took our coats off and held our faces to the sun. We walked along a side street to the park. No bombing here yet and the gardens were jaunty with lily-of-the-valley, tulips, and freesia. Wafts of the perfume from sweet peas and hyacinths led us forward, noses in the air. You could almost believe there was no war on.

We sat on a bench in the park and shared our sandwiches. 'Any news of your husband?' I asked Edith.

She inspected her sandwich which was beginning to curl at the edges, 'This is such a boring sandwich, don't know why I make them.'

'Remember rationing?' I said with a grin.

'Oh yes, rationing. No, haven't heard any more from him, but no news is good news as they say so I'm feeling good about him.'

We turned to Marian, 'What about your love life? You've been very quiet about that lately. Isn't your mum putting up some Canadian soldiers?'

Her cheeks burned red, 'Well, yes...'

Edith poked her arm, 'Yes, what? You got yourself a hunky Canadian?'

Marian bit her thumb nail. 'I've always liked one of them, Ethan. He's kind. Helps mum with the heavy lifting when the other blokes lay around all day smoking and dozing. Washes up sometimes too. And...'

This time we both prodded her, 'And...'

She gave a little smile, 'Well, he's got the front room for his bedroom. All the bedrooms upstairs are full. Mum always tells me to wake him up with a cup of tea.'

I grinned, 'So you go in there while he's still in his pyjamas?'

'That's tempting.' Edith said.

Marian bit her thumb nail again, 'We sort of, well...'

'You do it!' Edith squealed,

An elderly couple walked by and looked at us, their faces stony. I wondered if they guessed what Marian had done. We stopped speaking as if our tongues had been cut out. We watched their slow steps almost holding our breath, eager for more of the story.

Marian was nodding and biting her lip, her cheeks bright scarlet.

'What, you do it there and then with your mum in the house getting the breakfast ready?' I asked when the couple had gone out of earshot.

'I was so worried she'd hear, but Ethan said we could do it quietly.'

'So she hasn't twigged yet then? Got to admire your nerve.'

She looked from one of us to the other, 'That's it see, I'm a bag of nerves every time, but then I sort of...'

'Get overtaken by the moment?'

She cleared her throat, 'Yes, I suppose that's it. It's naughty, I know. I daren't confess when I go to church on Sundays.'

I handed her a sandwich, 'Go on, take my last sandwich as a token of my admiration. You're making both of you happy and who knows what the future will bring or even if we have a future.'

'Are you using Johnnies?' Edith asked.

The blush appeared again, 'Mmm, he uses them every time.'

'What about your little holiday?' Edith asked, turning to me, 'did you have a good time?'

It was my turn to blush, 'It was great, walking in the country, met a couple of airmen, spent the night with one of them.'

Edith choked so hard she spat out half her sandwich, 'You did what!'

I looked down at my hands, but couldn't stop a little smile lifting the edges of my mouth. 'Yes, met a smashing airman. Didn't do anyone any harm. My grandmother would turn in her grave if she knew. Anyway, I won’t be making a habit of it.’

Edith laughed, 'A lot of grannies must be turning in their graves these days.'

I decided not to give them any more details of my night with Richard, even though they begged. 'We went to a village fete and I won a bar of soap. Bronwyn told me how a magician there did a trick. It was a lovely few days away.'

I looked at my watch, 'Come on, girls, back to the grindstone.'

As we walked I thought about our conversation. Before the war no-one seemed to talk about sex, you'd think no-one ever did it. Most couples waited until they got married. Or said they did. But war changes attitudes.

Back at work I began to notice some mistakes in Mrs Rogan's paperwork. Sometimes a consignment would be marked in as complete, but when it was sent out to whoever ordered it, things got confusing and it looked like there'd be part of the order missing. I spent some time looking back through the dockets and other documents. It seemed to happen two or three times a week. Not huge amounts of anything. Maybe one case of corned beef or socks. By the end of the day I was no clearer and decided to speak to Mr McDonald about it the next time I saw him.

~

When I got back to our rooms there was Alun and to my amazement and delight he was wearing an army uniform. It may have been brand new but he still managed to make it look scruffy. His face was a picture, jaw jutting out, defiance blazing from his eyes as if he dared me to say anything. I stood looking at him; tried to speak but snorted laughter instead. I laughed so much I doubled over.

He glared at me and got a ciggie out of his pocket. 'Nothing to laugh about, cow,' he said, striking a match. The flare made his eyes narrow. 'I've got to report for duty tomorrow.'

Before I could answer Bronwyn walked in. She took one look at her brother and laughed as loudly as I did. His glare got fiercer. 'Don't know why I bothered coming to see you if you're going to be like that.'

Bronwyn wiped her eyes, 'Because you've got no-where else to go I expect. You won't have to worry about that any more, will you? Board and lodgings, all free, isn't it!'

He stood up, giving us death looks, 'I'm going to the pub, decent people to talk to there.' And with that, he stomped out the door, slamming it behind him.

Next day at work I went see Mr McDonald, the boss, first thing. Seeing I had an arm-full of papers he cleared a space on his desk for me to put them down, 'You look serious, Lily, sit down and tell me what's wrong.'

My stomach knotted and I twisted my hands together, wondering if I'd made a mistake and misunderstood what I'd been seeing. I didn't want him to think I was stupid.

'I'm probably wrong, but there seems to be some discrepancies in the paperwork I've been looking at.'

He frowned and leaned forward, 'Discrepancies? What sort of discrepancies? There's bound to be an occasional mistake.'

I picked up the top bits of paper I'd clipped together, 'It seems to be more than that; it's regular. Orders coming in and going out don't match. Have a look at these.'

I handed him the papers and showed him where I'd circled

the discrepancies. He took his time digesting the contents. 'And this is happening regularly, you say?'

'Not every day, more like two or three times a week. There must be someone in the yard involved, but I can't work out who.'

He stood up, 'Lily, if you're right, this is very difficult. Mrs Rogan has been with us for a long time and she's a valued member of staff.'

'But..'

He held up his hand, 'Don't think that means I won't take this seriously. I will. I'd like you to give me every document you have that relates to this. Then it's up to me to investigate further.'

I stood too, 'There's something else. The discrepancies stopped when Mrs Rogan went off sick.'

He sighed heavily, 'Oh dear, and I've noticed she never wanted to go on holiday. Please don't mention this to a soul, Lily. Let me deal with it and I promise you I will deal with it.'

'Why do you think she did it?' I asked, 'she seemed such an honest person.'

'Who knows?' he paused for a few seconds, 'I do know her brother has been ill for a long time. I wonder if it was so she could pay for his medical treatment.'

So many people couldn't afford to go to the doctor or the hospital. I thought how awful it must be to see your loved ones suffer because of lack of money.

I nodded and headed to the door. As I opened it he spoke again, 'Thank you for being so sharp eyed, Lily. We could do with more like you.'

I only wished it made me feel good instead of heavy hearted.

There had been no bombing for three nights. The air raid sirens still went off at six o'clock and people went to the shelters obediently the first couple of nights but on the third many stopped half way, 'Is it over? Do we really need to go?' Me and the other ARP wardens got asked again and again.

We couldn't know, but word was the Germans were too busy with their fight in Russia to keep bombing us. But there was no way of knowing if it was permanent. We still had to stick to our routines even though we were all dog tired from working all day and ARP volunteering some evenings each week. I had weekend leave due and decided to go home to Oxford to see Mum.

It was a cold day for May and I was glad of my ATS greatcoat to keep out the chill, especially when it started to drizzle. As usual the passenger trains were delayed while troop trains and goods trains got priority. As the minutes ticked past and the train got later and later passengers on the platform got edgy. Like me, many in uniform were on their precious weekend leave and every minute spent on the station platform was a minute less with their loved ones.

The station was packed by the time my train arrived and it was a mad rush to get on when the doors opened. People pushed each other out of the way and I even saw one soldier dive in through a window at the last moment. The carriage he landed in was full so without a word he climbed up onto the luggage rack, spread himself full length on it and went straight to sleep.

By the time the train pulled into Oxford, a weak sun had broken through and my great coat and rucksack seemed heavier. The station looked cheerful with the flower beds bright with Forget-me-nots, Gerbera and other flowers. Looking at my watch, I realised Mum would still be at work in the Munitions factory so decided to detour to the Dream Palace and see if my old boss was around, or any of the girls I worked with.

The row of shops before the Dream Palace were sad to see. Taylor's the butchers had three pork chops in their window display. He'd decorated them with a bit of parsley, but the empty metal trays aside them told the truth of wartime rationing. Ten or more women were queueing at Bright's the Bakers for their bread. Unlike most things bread wasn't rationed, but there was never enough to go round.

The Picture House looked just the same and I saw they were showing *Band Wagon* with Arthur Askey. I stood outside for a minute remembering that Edward and I had met at this very spot. A man snatched my bag and Edward got it back for me. So much had happened since then that it seemed like another life happening to someone else. Pushing open the glass and metal front door I was delighted that my old boss was standing there looking the same as ever.

'Lily!' he cried and rushed forward almost crushing me in a warm hug, 'let me look at you!' He pushed me away at arms length. 'Gorgeous as ever I see. And what a co-incidence that you should come today. Not an hour ago a soldier was looking for you.'

It seemed my heart stopped beating. 'A soldier? Did he tell you his name?'

He grinned, 'He did. It was Edward, your fiancé.'

I could hardly speak, 'Edward? Here? Where is he now?'

'He asked me if I knew where you were but of course I didn't know. I told him to try your mother's house.'

Without a word I ran out of the cinema and all the way home, sending up a breathless prayer over and over, 'Please let Edward still be there. Please let Edward still be there.' But I knew Mum would be at work so he wouldn't get any answer.

Out of breath, I almost collapsed at our gate when I saw Edward wasn't there. I'd long since given up hope of him being alive and now he was and we couldn't find each other.

I dropped my kitbag to the ground at the gate, and my shoulders sagged with disappointment. I decided that going to his parents' house was the best thing, but as I put my kitbag on my shoulder again Peggy from next door came out, 'You looking for your young man?' she asked, wiping her hands on her apron, 'He asked after you but I didn't know you were coming or I'd have told him to wait.'

Hope leapt in my chest again, 'Did he say where he was going?'

She nodded, 'Yes, said he was going to the station. You might catch him if you hurry, he's got a stick and he couldn't walk very fast.'

I handed her my rucksack and turned towards the station. I ran faster than I've ever run before, even in my army training days. A couple of times I got jokey comments from blokes I passed but this was no time to listen to them. It's strange how a journey can seem quick or slow, short or long, depending on your mood and circumstances. The journey back to the station, one I knew well, seemed twice as long as usual. I had to stop a couple of times because of a stitch in my side. Each time I saw a man in army uniform my heart soared, but it was never him.

I ran through the ticket office at the station, pushing people aside and looked around, but the platform was packed and at least three quarters of the men were in uniform. Frantic, I darted between people, looking for his lovely face. I searched for someone with a stick too and ran over to one man only to find when he turned round he was nothing like Edward. Desperate I shouted, 'EDWARD, EDWARD,' but as I did so a station announcement was made and my voice was drowned by news of the incoming train.

I dashed into the cafe in case he was there and peered through the cigarette fug hoping to see him; but no luck. I was just about to give up and was walking back towards the station entrance when the door to the Gents' opened and there he was, leaning heavily on a stick, pain etched on his face as he walked towards the train. I almost didn't recognise him because he looked so much thinner and his hair had a smattering of grey.

As I called his name, the station master made another announcement over the loud-speaker and a train chugged into the station. Edward hadn't heard me and I saw him pick up his bag and head towards the train. Yelling his name over and over I ran towards him and caught him as he stood aside to let passengers off the train.

He turned round and saw me. I hardly looked my best, sweating, with hair falling all over the place, but his eyes lit up. He dropped his bag and held out his arms. I fell into them, trying to catch my breath, 'Oh, Edward, Edward.' was all that I could manage to say.

We stood like that as people moved about us getting on and off trains. It was like we were waxwork figures amidst the living. Then Edward kissed the top of my head and I raised my face and we kissed deeply. All my worries about whether I'd still have feelings for him melted in that kiss and I felt safe and loved in his arms.

'Have you got to go now?' I asked when my brain began to work again. He shook his head,

'No, I was leaving because I couldn't find you, but I can

stay until tomorrow.' He held my hand, 'Come on, let's go back to the cafe, it's part of our history.'

The station cafe was as busy as ever and full of the smells of cooking and cigarettes. Edward walked with a noticeable limp, and I insisted he sit down while I get tea and buns. I didn't take my eyes off him the whole time I was queueing, worried he'd vanish into thin air and this was all a dream. I saw him flinch with pain as he sat down then he noticed me looking and adjusted his face to a smile.

When I eventually sat down he took my hands in his, 'I've been so worried Lily that you wouldn't want me after all this time. Especially now I've got this.' He tapped his gammy leg. 'You must have thought I was dead.'

I kissed his hands, my cheeks damp with tears. 'I did, I did, but I never quite gave up hope. Such a lot has happened since...' I thought about having been intimate with David and Richard and wondered if Edward would reject me because of it. There would never be anyone else for me now.

He put his finger to my lips, 'We have a lifetime to swap stories and you can't have done anything that would change my feelings for you.'

The tension in my shoulders relaxed, 'Nor mine for you. But where have you been Edward? We never heard a word.'

He tapped his stiff leg and then lifted his hair to show a scar on his scalp, 'I was knocked unconscious on duty in France and by the time I came round everyone had gone. Everyone living that is. A farmer came by on his horse and cart and took me in. For months they nursed me and I had no memory of anything. Nothing. I couldn't even remember who I was. The wound in my head and my leg injury stopped me leaving to find my regiment. We knew what that was from my uniform.'

'Oh, Edward, how awful for you, being ill and not knowing what was happening.'

He nodded, 'A lot of people have worse in this war and at least I'm still alive. The farmer didn't have a phone of course so there was no way to contact the regiment.'

I tried to imagine him there, alone and confused. I'd been through a lot since we parted but always had the comfort of Bronwyn and others around me.

'How did you get home? You must have been surrounded by the German army.'

'We were, and a few times they came to the farm and I had to pretend to be unconscious. His story was that I was his son and injured in an accident. That way I couldn't be asked questions when they'd soon realise I wasn't French. When I was strong enough Jacques, the farmer, made discrete inquiries of the resistance group. They smuggled me out through France and Spain to a ship back to Blighty. It took months especially as my walking is still pretty slow.'

'That must have been terrifying.'

He reached for my hand again, 'It was, I lost count of the number of times we thought we'd get caught, but the important thing is that we're here together now. My leg is slowly getting better.'

We sat, our tea getting cold, swapping stories and reaffirming our love. We had a lifetime ahead to build the future we wanted.

Once the war was over.

THE END

This is dedicated to my husband Rick, and my lovely family.

ACKNOWLEDGMENTS

So many people helped me bring this book from idea to reality. My husband, Rick, contributed many plot ideas - Nero's did a roaring trade in coffee as we discussed them. Also, thanks to the many friends who contributed ideas and/or proof read. They are: Joanna Lincoln, Pat Duckworth, Jacqui Kemp, Maggie Scott, Fran Johnstone (my writing buddy), Pauline Goss, Jane and Oliver Grieve

ABOUT THE AUTHOR

Patricia lives in Cambridge, UK, with her husband. She has written several self-help books and articles for national newspapers.

OTHER BOOKS BY PATRICIA MCBRIDE

FICTION

The Lily Baker Series:

The Picturehouse Girls

The Telephone Girls

The Deptford Girls

Standalone Books

Winner Takes All

Murder, Mystery & Magic

NON FICTION

How to be Assertive
Time Management for the Office
The Assertive Social Worker
The EI Advantage (with Susan Maitland)
CVs and Applications
Excel at Interviews
Study Skills for Success

Printed in Great Britain
by Amazon

56452196R00121